VANISHED CREATURES

Extinct Animals or Living Cryptids?

Mournheart Publishing

CONTENTS

INTRODUCTION TO CRYPTOZOOLOGY: FACT, FICTION, AND MYSTERY

C ryptozoology, the study of creatures whose existence is disputed or unverified by mainstream science, lies at the intersection of folklore, myth, and biological discovery. This field, often dismissed as pseudoscience, has long fascinated humanity with its tales of strange creatures—cryptids—that exist on the fringes of belief. From Bigfoot to the Loch Ness Monster, cryptozoologists investigate creatures for which there is anecdotal or circumstantial evidence but no definitive scientific proof.

However, cryptozoology isn't merely the study of mythical creatures. It's also a space where science and mystery collide, especially when it comes to animals thought to be extinct. This book explores a specific category of cryptids: creatures that were once believed to roam the Earth but are now presumed extinct. Could some of these vanished creatures still survive in remote areas, unnoticed by the scientific community?

The Origins of Cryptozoology

The term "cryptozoology" comes from the Greek words "kryptos" (hidden), "zoo" (animal), and "logos" (study). Although the term was coined in the mid-20th century, the fascination with unknown creatures dates back to ancient times. Ancient explorers and naturalists often returned from their travels with stories of strange and terrifying animals that had never been seen by their contemporaries. Many of these creatures were later discovered to be real, such as the Komodo dragon, the okapi, and the coelacanth —animals that were once thought to be mythical but were proven to exist through science.

Cryptozoology became more formalized in the 1950s through the work of Belgian-French zoologist Bernard Heuvelmans, whose book *On the Track of Unknown Animals* laid the foundation for the field. Heuvelmans emphasized the importance of studying folklore, indigenous knowledge, and historical accounts as valuable sources of evidence for the possible existence of unknown species.

Famous Cryptids

Many cryptids are creatures whose existence remains unverified by the scientific community, but they captivate the popular imagination. Bigfoot, the Yeti, and the Loch Ness Monster are some of the best-known examples. These creatures are often subjects of urban legend, media sensation, and controversy. While mainstream scientists often dismiss cryptids as products of misidentification or hoaxes, cryptozoologists argue that not all cryptid sightings can be so easily explained.

But cryptozoology isn't only about fantastical creatures. Some cryptids are creatures once known to science, like the Tasmanian Tiger or the Ivory-Billed Woodpecker, whose survival remains a possibility despite being declared extinct. These cases blur the line between myth and reality.

Extinct Animals as Cryptids

One of the most tantalizing aspects of cryptozoology is the possibility that some animals presumed extinct could still exist in isolated environments. Throughout history, animals have been rediscovered after long periods of absence, leading to the phenomenon known as "Lazarus taxa." For example, the coelacanth, a prehistoric fish thought to have gone extinct 66 million years ago, was found alive off the coast of South Africa in 1938.

In some cases, animals may persist in the wild but are mistaken for other species, or their populations are so small and isolated that they avoid detection. In other cases, animals may have gone extinct in one region while surviving in another, undisturbed by human activity. The key question cryptozoologists ask is: Could the same be true for other species that have vanished from official records?

Challenges in Proving the Existence of Cryptids

The pursuit of cryptids, especially creatures thought to be extinct, presents numerous challenges. Eyewitness accounts are often unreliable, and physical evidence such as photographs or footprints can be difficult to verify. In many cases, the habitats where cryptids are believed to exist are remote and inhospitable, making scientific expeditions difficult.

However, with advancements in technology, including DNA analysis and camera traps, cryptozoologists are finding new ways to search for elusive creatures. Discovering an animal thought to be extinct would not only rewrite our understanding of its history but also challenge the notion of extinction itself.

Purpose of This Book

This book will explore the stories of animals once declared extinct that may still survive as cryptids. Through historical records, scientific discoveries, and modern sightings, we'll examine the evidence for their continued existence and consider the possibility that the extinction of these creatures might not be as final as we once believed.

THE TASMANIAN TIGER: EXTINCT OR ELUSIVE SURVIVOR?

The Tasmanian Tiger, scientifically known as Thylacinus cynocephalus, was one of the most enigmatic creatures of the Australian wilderness. This carnivorous marsupial, also referred to as the Thylacine, once roamed the wilds of Tasmania, mainland Australia, and New Guinea. Famous for its distinct tiger-like stripes on its back, the Thylacine has become a symbol of lost wildlife, a reminder of how human intervention can lead to the tragic extinction of a species. But is it truly gone?

Despite being officially declared extinct in 1936, when the last known specimen died in captivity, the Tasmanian Tiger continues to capture imaginations around the world. For decades, sightings have been reported across Tasmania and mainland Australia, fueling speculation that small populations might still survive, hidden in the island's rugged wilderness. In this chapter, we will explore the fascinating history of the Tasmanian Tiger, the reasons for its supposed extinction, the numerous sightings that have sparked belief in its continued survival, and the scientific efforts to rediscover or even resurrect this iconic creature.

1. The Thylacine: A Brief Biological and Ecological Overview

The Tasmanian Tiger was the largest carnivorous marsupial of modern times. It is important to note that, despite its name, the Thylacine was not closely related to tigers or other big cats. It evolved as a marsupial predator, more closely related to kangaroos and koalas than to the felines of other continents. Its dog-like appearance, complete with a stiff tail and a large head, often led early European settlers to compare it to wolves or foxes, but the distinctive stripes on its lower back earned it the name "Tasmanian Tiger."

Physical Characteristics

Adult Thylacines measured about 100 to 130 cm in body length, with an additional 50 to 65 cm for their tail, and they stood approximately 60 cm at the shoulder. Their weight ranged from 15 to 30 kg, though some large males may have exceeded 35 kg. The Thylacine had short, coarse fur, typically light brown or yellowish-brown in color, with 13 to 21 dark stripes running across its back, which faded as they neared the tail. These stripes were one of its most distinguishing features, giving it a distinctly "tiger-like" appearance.

Another unique feature of the Thylacine was its pouch. Like many other marsupials, the females carried their young in a pouch. Interestingly, male Thylacines also had a rudimentary pouch that protected their external reproductive organs, a trait rare among marsupials.

The Thylacine's jaws were particularly interesting to scientists. Its wide gape allowed it to open its mouth to an impressive 80-degree angle, much wider than a dog or cat could. This feature gave the Thylacine an imposing look and allowed it to prey on animals larger than itself. However, its bite force was relatively weak for a predator of its size, leading researchers to believe that it may have relied more on scavenging than hunting.

Habitat and Behavior

The Thylacine was a nocturnal and semi-nocturnal hunter, mostly active at dusk and dawn. It favored forested and open scrubland habitats where it could stalk its prey in the cover of darkness. On Tasmania, it was known to inhabit the island's dense rainforests and coastal scrub areas. On mainland Australia, fossil evidence suggests that it once roamed across a wide range of environments, from arid deserts to eucalyptus woodlands.

Thylacines were solitary or paired animals, believed to live in family groups or as breeding pairs. Their diet primarily consisted of small to medium-sized mammals, birds, and possibly reptiles. The Thylacine was known to prey on kangaroos, wallabies, wombats, and bandicoots. There is also evidence to suggest that it scavenged carrion, which might explain its somewhat low bite force compared to other predators. This scavenging behavior may have been a vital survival strategy during periods when prey was scarce.

Although little is known about its social structure, indigenous Aboriginal rock art depicts Thylacines hunting in groups, leading some researchers to speculate that they may have coordinated during hunts, similar to modern-day wolves.

2. Early Human Contact and the Path to Extinction

The Thylacine once thrived across mainland Australia and New Guinea before its population became restricted to the island of Tasmania. The story of its extinction is deeply intertwined with the arrival of European settlers in Tasmania in the early 19th century.

Pre-European Impact: Aboriginal Rock Art and Mythology

Before European settlement, Thylacines were widely distributed across Australia. Fossil evidence suggests that they were present on the mainland until about 3,000 years ago, after which their range was limited to Tasmania. While the exact reasons for their disappearance from the mainland remain unclear, it is thought that competition with humans, along with the introduction of the dingo—a wild dog native to Australia—may have played a significant role. Dingoes, which arrived in Australia with humans around 4,000 years ago, outcompeted the Thylacine for prey and may have even preyed upon Thylacine pups.

Indigenous Australians were well aware of the Thylacine's presence, and their rock art provides one of the oldest visual records of the animal. These ancient depictions, found in caves across Northern Australia, show Thylacines in great detail, with their distinctive stripes and slender bodies. Aboriginal folklore and myths surrounding the Thylacine portray it as a powerful and mysterious creature, often feared for its strength and cunning. In some cultures, the Thylacine was revered as a spiritual animal, symbolizing the wild and untamed aspects of nature.

European Settlement and Conflict
The arrival of European settlers in Tasmania in 1803 marked the beginning of the end for the Thylacine. With settlers came a wave of environmental destruction. Large areas of Tasmania's native forests were cleared for agriculture, drastically reducing the Thylacine's natural habitat. Livestock farming, especially sheep farming, grew rapidly during this period, and the Thylacine soon found itself in direct conflict with farmers.

Although there is little hard evidence to suggest that Thylacines regularly attacked livestock, they were quickly labeled as a major threat to the farming industry. Farmers accused the Thylacine of preying on sheep and chickens, and it wasn't long before bounties were placed on their heads. The Tasmanian government introduced a bounty system in the late 19th century, offering rewards for killing Thylacines, and from 1888 to 1909, over 2,000 bounties were claimed.

Decline and Last Known Specimens
By the early 20th century, Thylacine numbers had plummeted. The combined impact of habitat loss, hunting, and competition with introduced species like dogs and foxes had decimated the population. Despite the bounty system being officially repealed in 1909, the damage was already done.

The last known wild Thylacine was shot by a farmer in 1930, and just six years later, the last captive Thylacine, named Benjamin, died at Hobart Zoo on September 7, 1936. Benjamin's death was a tragedy not only for the Thylacine but also for conservation efforts, as no formal breeding programs or attempts at preservation were ever initiated. Despite the extinction declaration, sightings and reports of Thylacines in the wild would continue to emerge, sparking one of the most enduring mysteries in the history of cryptozoology.

3. Sightings and Eyewitness Accounts
One of the most compelling aspects of the Thylacine's story is the sheer volume of reported sightings after it was declared extinct. From the mid-20th century through to today, there have been hundreds of reports of Thylacine sightings, primarily in Tasmania, but also on the Australian mainland and even in New Guinea.

Early Post-Extinction Sightings
Almost immediately after the species was declared extinct, people began reporting sightings of Thylacines in Tasmania's wilderness. These reports often described encounters with a large, striped, dog-like animal resembling the Thylacine. In the 1940s and 1950s, numerous bushmen, hunters, and tourists reported seeing Thylacines while exploring Tasmania's remote regions. Many of these reports came from the rugged and dense bushland of the island's western coast, where human activity was minimal.

In 1945, well-known naturalist and explorer David Fleay

conducted an expedition to investigate claims of a Thylacine sighting. Fleay's expedition found no hard evidence, but he remained convinced that the species was still out there. Similar expeditions followed, but none were able to capture concrete proof of the Thylacine's existence.

Modern Sightings

In recent decades, sightings of the Tasmanian Tiger have continued to be reported. Some of the most intriguing sightings occurred in the 1980s and 1990s, with eyewitnesses describing encounters remarkably similar to earlier reports. In many cases, these sightings involved people who were familiar with local wildlife, such as farmers, wildlife rangers, and experienced bushwalkers.

In 1982, a Park Ranger named Hans Naarding reported what is perhaps the most famous sighting. Naarding described seeing a Thylacine at close range during a nocturnal wildlife survey in northwestern Tasmania. According to Naarding, the animal was clearly visible in the beam of his spotlight for several minutes before it bolted into the underbrush. His report caused a stir, leading to a series of intensive searches, but no hard evidence was found.

Another notable sighting occurred in 1995 when a former tourism operator, Mary Robinson, claimed to have seen a Thylacine near a creek on the west coast of Tasmania. She described the animal in great detail, noting its distinctive stripes and its awkward gait, which matched historical descriptions of how the Thylacine moved.

More recently, in 2017, a document from the Department of Primary Industries, Parks, Water, and Environment (DPIPWE) in Tasmania revealed that there had been eight credible Thylacine sightings reported between 2016 and 2017. One of these reports came from a group of people traveling in a vehicle at night, who claimed to have seen a Thylacine cross the road. According to the report, the group described the animal's features in detail, including its striped hindquarters and stiff tail.

Photographic and Video Evidence

While eyewitness reports are plentiful, photographic and video evidence of the Thylacine remains scarce and highly contested. Several grainy photos and shaky videos have surfaced over the years, with some claiming to show Thylacines in the wild. However, most of these images have been either debunked as hoaxes or dismissed as misidentifications of other animals, such as foxes or wild dogs.

In 2016, footage of an alleged Thylacine filmed in southern Victoria (on the mainland) reignited interest in the species. The footage, captured by a man named Paul Day, showed a striped, dog-like animal walking through a field. However, experts who analyzed the video were divided, with some suggesting the animal was a large fox or a dog with a brindled coat, while others believed it was possibly a Thylacine.

Despite the lack of definitive photographic evidence, the sheer number of sightings and the consistency of descriptions have kept the mystery alive.

4. Scientific Efforts to Find or Revive the Thylacine

The persistence of Thylacine sightings has led to several organized expeditions to search for the animal, as well as modern scientific efforts to bring the species back from extinction.

Search Expeditions

Over the years, numerous expeditions have been launched to search for evidence of surviving Thylacines. One of the most well-known efforts was undertaken by naturalist Eric Guiler in the 1960s. Guiler, who spent much of his career studying the Thylacine, led several expeditions into Tasmania's wilderness to search for the elusive animal. While Guiler never found concrete evidence, he remained a firm believer that the Thylacine had survived.

In the 1980s, Australian magazine *The Bulletin* funded an expedition that offered a large reward for anyone who could provide verifiable proof of a living Thylacine. Despite generating significant public interest, the expedition failed to uncover any new evidence.

In 2005, the Thylacine Research Unit (TRU) was formed, consisting of researchers and cryptozoologists dedicated to finding proof of the Thylacine's existence. TRU has conducted numerous field surveys using camera traps and other modern technology, but to date, no definitive evidence has been produced.

Cloning and Genetic Research

In recent years, advances in genetic science have opened up the possibility of "de-extincting" the Tasmanian Tiger. In 1999, Australian scientists successfully extracted DNA from preserved Thylacine specimens, and efforts have been made to sequence its genome. These developments have led to discussions about cloning the Thylacine and bringing it back to life, similar to the projects aimed at reviving the Woolly Mammoth.

In 2021, researchers at the University of Melbourne made significant progress in sequencing the Thylacine's DNA, using specimens preserved in ethanol. While the project is still in its early stages, the potential to one day clone the Thylacine raises fascinating ethical questions about the future of de-extinction science.

5. Could the Tasmanian Tiger Still Survive?

The question that remains is: Could the Thylacine still be alive today? The possibility seems remote, yet not impossible. Tasmania's dense, rugged wilderness, particularly in the southwest, is largely uninhabited by humans and remains difficult to access. It is conceivable that small, isolated populations of Thylacines could persist in such environments, avoiding detection.

Supporters of the theory point to the existence of "Lazarus taxa," species once thought extinct that have been rediscovered, such as the Coelacanth and the Lord Howe Island stick insect. Could the Thylacine be another example of a species that defies extinction?

On the other hand, skeptics argue that if the Thylacine were still alive, some physical evidence—such as bones, scat, or carcasses—should have been found by now. Additionally, with the widespread use of camera traps and drones in modern wildlife research, the chances of capturing clear evidence of the Thylacine's existence should have increased, yet no such evidence has emerged.

Conclusion

The Tasmanian Tiger remains one of the most captivating creatures in the world of cryptozoology. While its extinction is widely accepted by the scientific community, the persistence of sightings and the enduring belief in its survival continue to inspire hope that one day, the Thylacine will be rediscovered. Whether hidden deep in Tasmania's wilderness or waiting to be revived through science, the legacy of the Tasmanian Tiger lives on, a symbol of both the fragility and the resilience of life.

THE WOOLLY MAMMOTH: IS THE ICE AGE TITAN STILL ALIVE?

T he Woolly Mammoth (Mammuthus primigenius) is an icon of the Ice Age, a towering beast that roamed the frigid landscapes of the northern hemisphere before mysteriously disappearing around 10,000 years ago. Despite the assumption that mammoths were wiped out by climate change and human hunting, stories and sightings of these giant creatures have persisted, particularly in the remote, frozen wilderness of Siberia.

Could the Woolly Mammoth still exist, surviving in isolated pockets of the Arctic tundra? Or are modern efforts to revive this prehistoric giant through cloning the only path to bringing the Woolly Mammoth back? In this chapter, we will explore the history of the Woolly Mammoth, its extinction, the scientific discoveries that have fueled modern mammoth hunts, and the extraordinary efforts to bring it back to life.

1. The Woolly Mammoth: An Ice Age Giant

The Woolly Mammoth was one of the largest land mammals of its time, standing up to 3.5 meters tall at the shoulder and weighing as much as 6 tons. It was closely related to modern elephants, particularly the Asian elephant, with whom it shared many physical and genetic similarities.

Physical Characteristics

Woolly Mammoths were uniquely adapted to the cold environments of the Ice Age, with their thick fur, a layer of insulating fat, and specialized blood proteins that helped them retain body heat. Their long, curved tusks, which could reach up to 15 feet in length, were used for foraging in the snow and for defense against predators. These tusks are one of the most distinctive features of the Woolly Mammoth, and fossilized tusks have been discovered across the northern hemisphere.

Mammoths also had large, humped shoulders due to the enormous muscles needed to support their heavy heads and tusks. Their ears were much smaller than those of modern elephants, an adaptation that minimized heat loss in cold climates. Additionally, they had specialized teeth for grinding coarse vegetation, their primary diet, which included grasses, sedges, and other Ice Age plants.

Habitat and Distribution

Woolly Mammoths were widespread across the northern hemisphere, ranging from North America and Europe to northern Asia. They thrived in the mammoth steppe, a vast, cold grassland that stretched across much of the Arctic during the Pleistocene epoch. These grasslands provided ample food for the mammoths, which grazed in large herds much like modern elephants.

Mammoths played a crucial ecological role in maintaining the health of the steppe. By grazing on vegetation and uprooting trees, they helped keep the landscape open and grass-dominated, which in turn supported a diverse range of other species, including large predators like sabertooth cats and dire wolves.

2. The Extinction of the Woolly Mammoth

The disappearance of the Woolly Mammoth around 10,000 years ago coincided with the end of the last Ice Age, a period of significant climate change that saw the Earth's temperatures rise and the glaciers retreat. This warming led to the gradual replacement of the cold, grassy steppe with forests and wetlands, environments less suited to mammoths.

Climate Change and Habitat Loss

As the Ice Age ended, the mammoth steppe—a critical habitat for Woolly Mammoths—began to shrink. Forests expanded northward, replacing the open grasslands that had supported mammoth populations for tens of thousands of years. The reduction of their habitat forced mammoths into increasingly smaller and more isolated pockets of the Arctic.

The changing climate also affected the availability of food. The tundra became wetter, and the types of vegetation that the mammoths relied on became less abundant. These environmental changes, combined with the pressures of human hunting, are believed to have driven the mammoth to the brink of extinction.

Human Hunting

Humans had a significant impact on mammoth populations. Archaeological evidence shows that early humans hunted Woolly Mammoths for food, clothing, and tools. Mammoth bones were used to build shelters, and their tusks were carved into weapons and art. Some researchers believe that human overhunting, combined with climate change, accelerated the extinction of mammoths.

Hunting pressure from humans may have been particularly devastating during the end of the Ice Age when mammoth populations were already struggling due to habitat loss. As the mammoth steppe disappeared, the surviving populations became more vulnerable to extinction.

The Last Mammoths: Wrangel Island

While most Woolly Mammoths went extinct around 10,000 years ago, a small population survived on Wrangel Island, an isolated landmass off the coast of Siberia. Remarkably, these mammoths persisted until around 4,000 years ago—long after the construction of the pyramids in Egypt.

The mammoths of Wrangel Island were smaller than their mainland relatives, possibly due to the limited resources available on the island. However, their isolation protected them from human hunters and environmental changes that affected the mainland populations. Despite this, the Wrangel Island mammoths eventually succumbed to a combination of genetic inbreeding and environmental shifts.

3. Reports of Modern Mammoths: Myths and Sightings

Despite their presumed extinction, rumors of surviving Woolly Mammoths have persisted for centuries, particularly in Siberia. Indigenous peoples in northern Russia have long told stories of encounters with large, hairy elephants roaming the remote tundra. These tales were often dismissed as folklore, but occasional sightings by explorers and hunters have kept the legend of the living mammoth alive.

Historical Reports and Expeditions

The earliest European reports of living mammoths date back to the 16th and 17th centuries when Russian explorers ventured into Siberia. Some of these explorers claimed to have seen large, hairy creatures resembling elephants. In 1806, a famous French naturalist, Georges Cuvier, argued that these sightings were based on the discovery of frozen mammoth carcasses preserved in Siberian permafrost. These well-preserved remains were often mistaken for living creatures.

However, in the 19th and early 20th centuries, reports of living mammoths continued to surface. In 1920, a Russian hunter named Mikhail Zhukov claimed to have seen a group of mammoths in the remote Siberian wilderness. His story was never verified, but it sparked a wave of interest in the possibility that isolated populations of mammoths might still exist.

In the 1940s and 1950s, several Soviet expeditions were launched to investigate claims of mammoth sightings in Siberia. These expeditions, while unsuccessful in finding any living mammoths, discovered numerous well-preserved carcasses buried in permafrost, further fueling speculation.

Modern Sightings
More recently, in the 21st century, reports of mammoth sightings have emerged from remote parts of Siberia. In 2011, a controversial video purportedly showing a living Woolly Mammoth crossing a river in the Chukotka region of Siberia was circulated online. The video, which was quickly debunked as a hoax, reignited public interest in the idea of surviving mammoths.

While these modern sightings are often dismissed by scientists, they highlight the enduring fascination with the Woolly Mammoth and the possibility that small, isolated populations could still exist in the vast, unexplored regions of Siberia.

4. De-Extinction: Bringing the Mammoth Back to Life
The Woolly Mammoth has become the poster child for the emerging field of de-extinction—the process of reviving extinct species using genetic engineering. Advances in genetic science have made it theoretically possible to bring the Woolly Mammoth back to life, raising profound ethical and ecological questions.

Cloning and Genetic Engineering
The first step in the de-extinction process is the sequencing of the

Woolly Mammoth's genome, which was completed in 2015 by a team of scientists led by Dr. George Church at Harvard University. Using DNA extracted from well-preserved mammoth remains, the team successfully mapped the genetic code of the mammoth, providing the blueprint for potential cloning efforts.

However, cloning an extinct animal is a complex and challenging process. To revive the Woolly Mammoth, scientists would need to insert mammoth DNA into the egg of a closely related species —likely an Asian elephant—and use the elephant as a surrogate mother. This process, known as somatic cell nuclear transfer, has been used to clone other animals, such as sheep and horses, but it has never been attempted with an extinct species.

In addition to cloning, researchers are exploring the possibility of editing the genes of Asian elephants to give them mammoth-like traits. By inserting genes responsible for cold adaptation, such as those that control hair growth and fat storage, scientists hope to create a hybrid species—a "mammophant"—that would closely resemble the Woolly Mammoth.

Ethical and Ecological Considerations
While the prospect of reviving the Woolly Mammoth is scientifically exciting, it raises several ethical and ecological concerns. One of the primary questions is whether it is appropriate to bring back a species that has been extinct for thousands of years. Some argue that de-extinction could divert resources away from conserving endangered species and habitats.

Another concern is the potential ecological impact of reintroducing mammoths into modern ecosystems. The Arctic has changed significantly since the end of the Ice Age, and it is unclear how mammoths would fit into today's tundra environment. Proponents of de-extinction, however, argue that reintroducing mammoths could help restore the mammoth steppe and combat climate change by promoting the growth of grasses that sequester carbon.

5. Could the Mammoth Still Be Alive?

While the idea of surviving Woolly Mammoths is tantalizing, the likelihood of their existence today is slim. The vast expanses of Siberia remain largely unexplored, but the discovery of so many well-preserved mammoth carcasses suggests that if living populations existed, we would have found stronger evidence by now.

However, the search for living mammoths continues to captivate the public imagination, and the possibility of reviving the species through science keeps the dream of the Woolly Mammoth alive. Whether through discovery or de-extinction, the Woolly Mammoth may yet walk the Earth again.

THE IVORY-BILLED WOODPECKER: A GHOST IN THE FORESTS

The Ivory-Billed Woodpecker (Campephilus principalis) was once a magnificent bird of the southern United States' swampy forests. With its striking black-and-white plumage, large size, and ivory-colored bill, it was an iconic symbol of the deep, unspoiled wilderness. But after decades of deforestation and human encroachment, the Ivory-Billed Woodpecker was declared extinct in the mid-20th century. However, like many creatures thought to be lost, the Ivory-Billed Woodpecker has refused to fade quietly into the annals of history. Despite its official extinction status, there have been persistent reports of sightings and auditory recordings, sparking hope that this ghost of the forest might still exist.

In this chapter, we will explore the history of the Ivory-Billed Woodpecker, the reasons for its decline, the various expeditions launched to find it, and the tantalizing evidence that suggests it might still be out there, deep in the forests of the American South.

1. The Ivory-Billed Woodpecker: A Regal Bird

The Ivory-Billed Woodpecker was the largest woodpecker in North America, reaching lengths of 18 to 20 inches with a wingspan of nearly 30 inches. Its distinctive black-and-white plumage, combined with its striking ivory-colored bill, made it one of the most visually impressive birds of the American wilderness. The males also sported a brilliant red crest, adding to their majestic appearance.

Habitat and Behavior

Ivory-Billed Woodpeckers were native to the old-growth swamp forests of the southeastern United States, including the bayous of Louisiana, the hardwood forests of Florida, and the bottomlands of Arkansas. These forests provided the ideal environment for the bird's specialized foraging behavior, as it relied on dead and dying trees to find its primary food source: beetle larvae.

Ivory-Billed Woodpeckers were known for their powerful beaks, which they used to excavate deep into tree bark to extract insects. They would hammer away at trees with a distinctive double-knock sound, which became a signature of their presence. This sound, along with their striking appearance, made them easy to identify for those lucky enough to encounter them.

The Decline of the Ivory-Billed Woodpecker

The decline of the Ivory-Billed Woodpecker began in the late 19th century, as vast swaths of its forested habitat were cleared for agriculture and logging. The bird's reliance on large tracts of undisturbed forest made it particularly vulnerable to deforestation, and by the early 20th century, it was already becoming rare. The last confirmed sighting of an Ivory-Billed Woodpecker occurred in 1944 in the Singer Tract, a large forest in Louisiana that was subsequently logged, further reducing the bird's habitat.

Despite its rarity, there was little concerted effort to protect the Ivory-Billed Woodpecker at the time. Conservation was still in its infancy in the early 20th century, and the bird's decline went largely unnoticed by the general public. By the time scientists and conservationists realized the severity of the situation, it was too late.

2. The Search for the Ivory-Billed Woodpecker

Despite its official extinction status, rumors of surviving Ivory-Billed Woodpeckers have persisted for decades. These reports, often coming from remote and difficult-to-access areas, have inspired numerous expeditions to search for the elusive bird.

The 2004 Rediscovery

In 2004, an ornithologist named David Luneau captured a few seconds of video footage that reignited hope for the survival of the Ivory-Billed Woodpecker. Luneau was part of a team of researchers from Cornell University who had been searching for the bird in the Cache River National Wildlife Refuge in Arkansas. The grainy video, which showed a large woodpecker with the distinctive black-and-white pattern of the Ivory-Bill, was hailed as proof that the bird was still alive.

The news of the rediscovery caused a sensation in the birding community and beyond. The U.S. government allocated millions of dollars to support conservation efforts in the area, and the Ivory-Billed Woodpecker became a symbol of hope for the survival of other endangered species. However, not everyone was convinced. Some ornithologists argued that the bird in Luneau's video could have been a Pileated Woodpecker, a similar species that is still relatively common in the southeastern U.S.

Despite extensive searches in the years that followed, no conclusive evidence of a surviving population of Ivory-Billed Woodpeckers was found. The bird remains listed as critically endangered, and the question of whether it still exists remains unresolved.

Other Sightings and Recordings

In addition to the 2004 Arkansas sighting, there have been numerous other reports of Ivory-Billed Woodpeckers in recent years. Some of these reports come from the Florida panhandle, where large areas of old-growth forest still remain. In 2005, a team of researchers from Auburn University claimed to have heard the distinctive double-knock sound of an Ivory-Billed Woodpecker in the Choctawhatchee River basin. Audio recordings from the area captured what some experts believe could be the drumming of a surviving Ivory-Bill.

Other sightings have been reported in Louisiana, Texas, and South Carolina. However, like the Arkansas sighting, these reports have been met with skepticism, and none have provided definitive proof of the bird's existence.

3. The Ivory-Billed Woodpecker: A Ghost in the Forest?

The search for the Ivory-Billed Woodpecker has taken on an almost mythic quality, with birders and ornithologists venturing into the deep swamps and forests of the American South in search of a creature that might not exist. The persistence of sightings, despite the lack of hard evidence, has led some to view the Ivory-Bill as a symbol of humanity's yearning to undo the damage we have done to the natural world.

Ecological Importance

The Ivory-Billed Woodpecker played a crucial role in its ecosystem as both a predator of insects and a creator of habitat for other species. By excavating dead trees in search of food, Ivory-Billed Woodpeckers created cavities that were used by other birds, mammals, and reptiles for nesting and shelter. The loss of the Ivory-Bill has likely had cascading effects on the ecosystems where it once lived.

The bird also served as an indicator of the health of old-growth forests. Its presence signaled that a forest was relatively undisturbed, with plenty of dead and dying trees to support its specialized foraging habits. The disappearance of the Ivory-Billed Woodpecker is a reminder of the fragility of these ecosystems and the consequences of human activity.

4. Could the Ivory-Billed Woodpecker Survive?

The question of whether the Ivory-Billed Woodpecker still exists is one of the great mysteries of modern ornithology. The bird's habitat, once vast and unspoiled, has been reduced to a fraction of its original size. However, there are still areas of remote, inaccessible forest in the southeastern U.S. where a small population of Ivory-Bills could potentially survive undetected.

Proponents of the bird's survival argue that the Ivory-Bill's elusive nature, combined with the difficulty of accessing its remaining habitat, makes it possible that a small population has persisted. Critics, however, point to the lack of concrete evidence and the fact that so many searches have failed to turn up anything definitive.

5. Conclusion: The Legacy of the Ivory-Billed Woodpecker

Whether or not the Ivory-Billed Woodpecker still survives, its story has captured the imagination of bird lovers, conservationists, and scientists alike. The bird's decline and possible extinction serve as a poignant reminder of the impact of human activity on the natural world, while the ongoing search for the Ivory-Bill offers a glimmer of hope that we may one day rediscover what was lost.

THE MEGALODON: ANCIENT PREDATOR OR OCEAN PHANTOM?

T he Megalodon (Carcharocles megalodon) was one of the most fearsome predators to ever swim the oceans, a giant prehistoric shark that could grow up to 60 feet in length and had jaws powerful enough to crush whale bones. Though the Megalodon went extinct millions of years ago, stories and sightings of massive sharks far larger than any known species have led some to believe that this ancient predator might still lurk in the depths of the ocean.

In this chapter, we will dive into the history of the Megalodon, its role as an apex predator in prehistoric oceans, the reasons for its extinction, and the modern-day reports of Megalodon-like creatures. Could the Megalodon still exist, hiding in the unexplored depths of our oceans? Or are these reports merely cases of mistaken identity or exaggeration?

1. The Megalodon: Apex Predator of the Ancient Seas

The Megalodon was a giant shark that lived between 23 million and 3.6 million years ago, during the Miocene and Pliocene epochs. It was the largest predator to ever swim the oceans, and its size and strength made it a dominant force in marine ecosystems.

Physical Characteristics
Megalodons were enormous, with the largest individuals reaching lengths of up to 60 feet—three times the size of a modern Great White Shark. Their massive jaws were lined with serrated teeth, each up to 7 inches long, designed to tear through the flesh and bones of their prey. The Megalodon's bite force is estimated to have been between 10.8 and 18.2 tons, far greater than that of any other known animal, living or extinct.

These sharks had a robust, muscular body, similar in shape to modern Great Whites, but far larger. They were built for power rather than speed, likely relying on ambush tactics to take down large prey such as whales, dolphins, and other marine mammals.

Habitat and Range
Megalodons were cosmopolitan predators, meaning they could be found in oceans all over the world. Fossilized teeth have been discovered on every continent except Antarctica, indicating that Megalodons were able to adapt to a wide range of marine environments, from shallow coastal waters to the open ocean.

Megalodons likely preferred warmer waters, as their fossils are most commonly found in regions that were once tropical or subtropical. However, their wide distribution suggests that they were highly adaptable and capable of surviving in various oceanic conditions.

2. The Extinction of the Megalodon
The Megalodon went extinct around 3.6 million years ago, but the reasons for its extinction remain a topic of scientific debate. Several factors likely contributed to the demise of this ancient predator.

Climate Change

One of the primary drivers of the Megalodon's extinction was climate change. As the Earth's climate cooled during the late Pliocene, sea levels dropped, and the warm, shallow seas that Megalodons favored began to disappear. The cooling oceans also affected the distribution of the Megalodon's prey, particularly marine mammals like whales, which migrated to colder waters where Megalodons could not easily follow.

Competition with Other Predators

At the same time, new predators emerged that may have outcompeted the Megalodon for food. The ancestors of modern Great White Sharks appeared around this time, and while much smaller than the Megalodon, they were more agile and better suited to the changing marine environment. Some scientists believe that Great Whites may have filled the ecological niche left by the Megalodon after its extinction.

Decline in Prey Populations

The decline of large marine mammals, particularly baleen whales, also contributed to the Megalodon's extinction. As global temperatures cooled, many species of whales migrated to colder waters, leaving the Megalodon with fewer prey options. Additionally, the extinction of smaller species of marine mammals may have reduced the availability of food for juvenile Megalodons, making it difficult for them to survive to adulthood.

3. Modern Sightings of Megalodon-like Creatures

Despite its presumed extinction, stories and reports of massive sharks far larger than any known species have persisted for centuries. These reports have fueled speculation that the Megalodon might still exist, lurking in the unexplored depths of the ocean.

Historical Accounts

Historical accounts of giant sharks date back to ancient times. Greek and Roman writers occasionally mentioned encounters with massive sea creatures, though it is unclear whether these descriptions referred to actual animals or were exaggerations or myths. In more recent centuries, sailors and fishermen have reported seeing sharks much larger than any known species.

One of the most famous early accounts comes from the 1800s when a British ship allegedly encountered a shark measuring over 100 feet in length off the coast of South Africa. While this story is widely regarded as an exaggeration, it highlights the enduring fascination with the possibility of giant sharks surviving into modern times.

The Black Demon of the Sea

One of the most well-known modern legends of a Megalodon-like creature comes from the waters off Baja California, where fishermen have reported sightings of a massive black shark, known as "The Black Demon." Descriptions of this creature vary, but it is often said to be 50 to 60 feet long, with a dark coloration and a fin that rises high above the water's surface.

While no physical evidence has been found to support the existence of the Black Demon, the stories have persisted for decades, and the creature has become a popular subject of cryptozoology and marine folklore.

Giant Shark Sightings

In recent years, there have been numerous reports of exceptionally large sharks, particularly Great Whites, being spotted by fishermen and marine biologists. Some of these sightings involve sharks that are far larger than the average size of a Great White, leading to speculation that these individuals might be descendants of the Megalodon or a previously unknown species.

One of the most famous examples is a Great White Shark nicknamed "Deep Blue," which was filmed off the coast of Hawaii in 2013. Deep Blue measures over 20 feet in length, making her one of the largest Great Whites ever recorded. While Deep Blue is not a Megalodon, her size has reignited public interest in the possibility of giant sharks surviving in modern oceans.

4. Could the Megalodon Still Exist?
The idea that the Megalodon could still exist in the unexplored depths of the ocean is an intriguing one, but most scientists remain skeptical. The ocean is vast and largely unexplored, with an estimated 80% of it remaining unmapped and unobserved. It is possible that undiscovered species still exist in the deep sea, but the likelihood of a creature as large as the Megalodon surviving undetected is slim.

One of the main arguments against the survival of the Megalodon is the lack of physical evidence. If a population of Megalodons still existed, we would expect to find teeth, bones, or carcasses washing up on beaches or being discovered by deep-sea explorers. Additionally, a creature as large as the Megalodon would require a massive amount of food, and it is unlikely that the modern ocean could support such a predator without leaving significant ecological evidence.

5. The Legacy of the Megalodon
While the Megalodon may no longer exist, its legacy lives on in popular culture and the scientific fascination with giant predators. The Megalodon has been the subject of countless books, movies, and documentaries, and its fearsome reputation continues to capture the imagination of people around the world. The search for the Megalodon, whether through cryptozoology or scientific discovery, reflects humanity's enduring fascination with the unknown and the possibility that the natural world still holds mysteries waiting to be uncovered.

THE MOA AND NEW ZEALAND'S LOST GIANTS

New Zealand's landscape once hosted a variety of giant flightless birds, the most famous of which was the Moa. These incredible, ostrich-like creatures, which could grow up to 12 feet tall and weigh more than 500 pounds, vanished around 500 to 600 years ago. However, legends, anecdotal sightings, and footprints have sparked speculation that some Moa might still roam the country's remote wilderness areas. Could these massive birds, hunted to extinction by the Maori, still exist today in isolated pockets?

In this chapter, we will explore the Moa's biology, their crucial role in New Zealand's ecosystems, the factors leading to their extinction, and modern reports that suggest they might still survive. The Moa stands as a key figure in cryptozoology and a symbol of the mysterious lost megafauna of the world.

1. The Moa: Giants of the Forest and Grasslands

Moa were flightless birds native to New Zealand, belonging to the family *Dinornithiformes*. There were nine species of Moa, ranging in size from smaller species, such as the Bush Moa, to the colossal

South Island Giant Moa, which was the tallest bird species ever known.

Physical Characteristics
The largest species of Moa, the South Island Giant Moa (*Dinornis robustus*), could reach up to 12 feet in height, with the males being much smaller than females—a rare trait known as sexual dimorphism. These towering birds had long necks and sturdy legs, similar to ostriches, and were completely flightless due to their lack of wing bones. Their diet consisted primarily of leaves, twigs, and other vegetation, which they foraged from trees and low bushes. Moa had powerful beaks and a unique digestive system, including gizzard stones, to help process the tough fibrous plants they consumed.

Moa feathers were relatively simple, providing protection against New Zealand's temperate climate. While their size and appearance may have made them seem invincible, Moa were vulnerable due to their inability to escape quickly from predators or human hunters.

Ecosystem Role
Moa played a pivotal role in shaping New Zealand's ecosystems. As herbivores, they were important seed dispersers and helped control the growth of forests and shrublands. Their browsing behavior significantly influenced the structure of New Zealand's vegetation, creating open grasslands and preventing forests from becoming too dense.

The extinction of Moa caused widespread ecological shifts. Without these large herbivores, the balance between plant species changed, and some plants that relied on Moa for seed dispersal experienced declines. In the wake of the Moa's disappearance, the ecosystem underwent a radical transformation, with certain bird species adapting to fill their ecological roles.

2. The Arrival of Humans and the Moa's Extinction

Before humans arrived in New Zealand, the Moa had no natural predators, allowing them to flourish for millions of years. However, that all changed when the Polynesian ancestors of the Maori arrived around 1300 AD.

Maori Hunting and Cultural Impact

The Maori settlers were skilled hunters who quickly adapted to their new environment. With no large land mammals on New Zealand, the Moa provided an abundant source of meat, feathers, and bones. Moa were hunted extensively, not just for food, but also for their bones, which were used to create tools, and their feathers, which were prized for ceremonial cloaks.

Within a few hundred years, overhunting led to the rapid extinction of all nine species of Moa. The exact timeline is debated, but most researchers agree that the Moa population collapsed by around 1440 AD. The extinction of the Moa is a classic example of human overexploitation driving a species to extinction.

Habitat Destruction

In addition to hunting, early Maori settlers burned large areas of New Zealand's forests to clear land for agriculture. This widespread habitat destruction further hastened the decline of the Moa, as their feeding grounds were reduced, and they were forced into increasingly fragmented environments.

3. Modern Sightings and Evidence for Survival

Despite their official extinction, stories of surviving Moa have persisted for centuries. New Zealand's rugged and remote wilderness areas, particularly the South Island's Fiordland and the West Coast's dense rainforests, are prime candidates for undiscovered wildlife. Eyewitness accounts, unexplained footprints, and other forms of evidence have led some to believe that Moa might still survive in these uninhabited regions.

Early 20th-Century Sightings

The first notable modern Moa sighting occurred in 1878 when an explorer named Richard Henry reported seeing a large, ostrich-like bird in the remote forests of Fiordland. Henry, a well-respected naturalist, claimed that the bird he saw was much larger than any known species of New Zealand birds. His sighting inspired further investigations, but no concrete evidence was found at the time.

In the 1920s, Australian adventurer and naturalist Geoffrey Orbell led several expeditions into the South Island's rainforests after hearing local rumors of surviving Moa. Orbell's expeditions were well-publicized, and he claimed to have seen large footprints in the mud, which he believed belonged to Moa. Unfortunately, Orbell was unable to find conclusive proof, though his stories fueled further searches.

Footprints and Modern Expeditions

In 1993, a team of researchers led by cryptozoologist Rex Gilroy claimed to have discovered fresh Moa footprints in Fiordland. These footprints, measuring 10 inches long, were far too large to belong to any known living bird species. Photographs and plaster casts of the prints were made, but the evidence was inconclusive, as some skeptics suggested the prints could have been made by emus or other birds.

More recently, in 2007, a hiker in the Craigieburn Range of the South Island reported seeing a large bird resembling a Moa. The sighting was brief, and no physical evidence was collected, but the hiker's description matched that of a Moa rather than any known species of bird. Such sightings have reignited interest in the possibility that small populations of Moa may have survived undetected in New Zealand's remote wilderness.

DNA and Cryptozoological Studies

In recent years, advances in DNA analysis have allowed scientists to extract and study Moa DNA from well-preserved fossils and subfossils. While there is no direct evidence of living Moa, researchers are using this genetic material to better understand the biology and evolution of the species.

Some cryptozoologists have suggested that using DNA technology, such as environmental DNA (eDNA) sampling, could help detect traces of Moa in the environment. This technique involves collecting samples from soil, water, or air and analyzing them for traces of DNA left behind by living organisms. If Moa are still alive, this method could potentially offer the proof that has eluded researchers for decades.

4. Could Moa Still Survive?

While the idea of surviving Moa is tantalizing, most scientists remain skeptical. The primary argument against the continued existence of Moa is the lack of physical evidence—no bodies, bones, or nests have been discovered in recent history. Additionally, Moa were large, slow-moving animals that would be difficult to overlook, even in New Zealand's dense forests.

However, proponents of the survival theory point to the vast, uninhabited regions of New Zealand's wilderness as potential refuges for small, isolated populations. They argue that if other large, flightless birds like the Kakapo (a nocturnal parrot) can survive undetected in remote areas, it is not impossible that Moa could have done the same.

5. Conclusion: The Mystery of the Moa

Whether or not the Moa still exists, its story is a cautionary tale of human impact on wildlife and the fragility of ecosystems. The extinction of the Moa altered New Zealand's landscape forever, and the ongoing search for surviving Moa highlights our enduring fascination with lost species. As cryptozoologists continue to explore New Zealand's wilderness, the possibility that these giants of the forest may yet be rediscovered keeps the legend of the Moa alive.

THE BAIJI DOLPHIN: CAN A RIVER GHOST RETURN?

The Baiji dolphin (Lipotes vexillifer), once known as the "Goddess of the Yangtze," was a freshwater dolphin species native to China's Yangtze River. Sadly, in 2006, the Baiji was declared functionally extinct after extensive surveys failed to find any living individuals. However, sporadic reports of Baiji sightings have continued to emerge, leading some to hope that a small population might still survive.

In this chapter, we will examine the biology of the Baiji, the factors that led to its near-extinction, and the efforts to protect it. We will also explore the possibility of the Baiji's return and whether it could once again swim through the waters of the Yangtze.

1. The Baiji: A Unique Freshwater Dolphin

The Baiji was a small, light-colored dolphin that inhabited the Yangtze River for millions of years. It was one of only four species of freshwater dolphins and was highly adapted to life in the turbid waters of the river.

Physical Characteristics and Behavior

Baiji dolphins were small compared to their marine relatives, typically measuring around 6 to 8 feet in length and weighing 250 to 500 pounds. They had a distinctive long, narrow snout that was perfect for catching fish, and their pale blue-gray skin made them difficult to spot in the murky waters of the Yangtze.

Baiji were known for their gentle nature and were often referred to as "Goddesses" by local fishermen. These dolphins had poor eyesight, relying on echolocation to navigate and find prey in the sediment-laden river. They primarily fed on fish, which they caught using quick, agile movements.

Baiji were highly social animals, often seen swimming in pairs or small groups. Their graceful swimming and gentle demeanor made them a beloved symbol of the Yangtze River's biodiversity.

2. The Decline of the Baiji: A Tragic Story of Human Impact

The Baiji's population began to decline rapidly in the second half of the 20th century as China's industrialization and population growth transformed the Yangtze River. The construction of dams, increased river traffic, and pollution all contributed to the dolphin's demise.

Industrialization and Habitat Destruction

The Baiji's habitat, the middle and lower reaches of the Yangtze River, became increasingly degraded as China underwent rapid industrialization. The construction of the Three Gorges Dam, one of the world's largest hydroelectric dams, significantly altered the river's flow, affecting fish populations and reducing the Baiji's access to food.

Additionally, increased shipping traffic on the Yangtze caused more frequent collisions between boats and Baiji, resulting in numerous injuries and deaths. The noise from boat engines also interfered with the dolphins' echolocation abilities, making it difficult for them to navigate and find food.

Overfishing and Bycatch
As human populations along the Yangtze grew, so did fishing activities. Overfishing depleted the Baiji's primary food sources, and many Baiji were accidentally caught in fishing nets as bycatch. These entanglements were often fatal, as the dolphins were unable to surface for air once trapped in the nets.

Pollution
Industrial pollution and agricultural runoff also took a heavy toll on the Yangtze's ecosystem. Toxic chemicals and heavy metals, along with untreated sewage, contaminated the river, affecting both the Baiji and their prey. High levels of pollution weakened the dolphins' immune systems, making them more susceptible to disease.

3. The 2006 Survey: Declaring the Baiji Functionally Extinct
In 2006, an international team of scientists conducted an extensive survey of the Yangtze River, searching for any remaining Baiji dolphins. The survey, which covered over 2,000 miles of the river, used advanced acoustic equipment to detect the dolphins' echolocation clicks.

Despite their best efforts, the team failed to find a single Baiji. Based on these results, the species was declared functionally extinct, meaning that even if a few individuals remained, they were not enough to sustain a viable breeding population. The Baiji became the first cetacean species to be driven to extinction by human activity.
The extinction of the Baiji was a sobering reminder of the impact that human development can have on vulnerable species, particularly those that rely on freshwater habitats.

4. Hopes for Survival: Recent Sightings and Conservation Efforts
Despite the 2006 declaration, there have been sporadic reports

of Baiji sightings in recent years, raising hopes that a small population might still survive.

Post-2006 Sightings

In 2007, just one year after the Baiji was declared extinct, a Chinese man claimed to have seen a live Baiji in the Yangtze River. His sighting was supported by video footage, though the quality was poor, and experts were divided on whether the animal in the video was indeed a Baiji.

In 2016, another potential sighting occurred when a group of fishermen reported seeing a dolphin-like creature swimming in the Yangtze. The fishermen, who were familiar with the Baiji from years of working on the river, believed the animal was a surviving Baiji. However, no definitive evidence was collected, and the sighting remains unverified.

These reports, while encouraging, have not been enough to convince scientists that the Baiji is still alive. The Yangtze River remains a highly degraded environment, and if any Baiji do survive, they are likely facing enormous challenges in terms of food availability and breeding opportunities.

Conservation Efforts

In the wake of the Baiji's extinction, conservation efforts have shifted toward protecting other endangered species in the Yangtze, such as the critically endangered Yangtze Finless Porpoise. This small cetacean is closely related to the Baiji and faces many of the same threats, including habitat loss and pollution.

Efforts to restore the health of the Yangtze River ecosystem, including reducing pollution and regulating fishing practices, may also benefit any surviving Baiji. However, given the extensive damage to the river, some conservationists argue that more drastic measures, such as creating artificial breeding habitats, may be necessary to ensure the survival of the Yangtze's remaining aquatic species.

5. Could the Baiji Dolphin Return?

The possibility of the Baiji's return remains uncertain. While the recent sightings offer a glimmer of hope, the challenges facing any surviving Baiji are immense. The Yangtze River continues to be heavily impacted by human activities, and even if a few Baiji still exist, their chances of long-term survival are slim without significant intervention.

Some researchers have proposed the idea of using cloning or assisted reproduction techniques to bring the Baiji back from extinction. While these technologies are still in their infancy, they offer a potential solution for restoring lost species, particularly those that have gone extinct in recent memory.

6. Conclusion: The Tragedy of the Baiji

The story of the Baiji dolphin is one of tragedy and loss, a reminder of the devastating impact that human development can have on wildlife. While the Baiji's extinction is a stark warning, it also serves as a call to action for the protection of other endangered species and the preservation of fragile ecosystems. Whether the Baiji can return or not, its legacy will continue to inspire conservation efforts around the world.

THE DODO: A BIRD GONE FOREVER, OR JUST FORGOTTEN?

T he Dodo (Raphus cucullatus) is perhaps the most famous extinct animal in history, a flightless bird that lived on the island of Mauritius in the Indian Ocean. Its extinction in the late 17th century, just a few decades after it was first encountered by European sailors, has become a symbol of human-induced extinction. However, the Dodo's story is more complex than the simple narrative of human hunting driving a species to extinction. Recent research and modern-day sightings of large, flightless birds in the region have led some to question whether the Dodo might still exist in some form.

In this chapter, we will explore the history of the Dodo, the factors that led to its extinction, and the tantalizing clues that suggest it might not be as extinct as we once believed.

1. The Dodo: An Island Giant

The Dodo was a large, flightless bird that lived on the island of Mauritius, located in the Indian Ocean. It belonged to the pigeon family and was closely related to other island-dwelling pigeons, such as the Nicobar pigeon.

Physical Characteristics and Behavior

The Dodo was a large bird, standing about 3 feet tall and weighing around 20 to 40 pounds. It had a plump, rounded body, short legs, and a large, hooked beak. Despite its ungainly appearance, the Dodo was well adapted to life on Mauritius, where it had no natural predators and abundant food sources, including fruits, seeds, and small invertebrates.

The Dodo's flightlessness was a result of its island habitat, where the lack of predators made flight unnecessary. Like many island species, the Dodo evolved to become larger and more sedentary than its mainland relatives. It likely spent much of its time foraging on the forest floor, using its powerful beak to crack open hard-shelled fruits.

The Dodo's behavior and social structure are not well understood, as it disappeared before detailed scientific observations could be made. However, based on the behavior of other flightless birds, it is believed that Dodos were social animals, living in small groups or pairs.

2. The Arrival of Humans and the Dodo's Extinction

The extinction of the Dodo is a classic example of the destructive impact that humans and introduced species can have on island ecosystems. Before the arrival of humans, Mauritius was a pristine, isolated environment, home to a variety of unique species, including the Dodo.

European Exploration and Hunting

The first recorded sighting of the Dodo was in 1598, when a group of Dutch sailors landed on Mauritius. The sailors described the bird as slow, tame, and easy to catch, leading them to give it the name "Dodo," derived from the Portuguese word "doudo," meaning "fool" or "simpleton."

The Dodo's lack of fear of humans made it an easy target for hunters. Although early accounts suggest that the bird's meat was tough and unpalatable, it was still hunted for food by sailors and settlers. The Dodo's large size and inability to fly made it particularly vulnerable to overhunting.

Introduced Species and Habitat Destruction
While hunting played a role in the Dodo's extinction, it was the introduction of invasive species that sealed the bird's fate. The Dutch settlers brought with them pigs, rats, and monkeys, all of which preyed on the Dodo's eggs and young. These introduced species quickly spread across the island, devastating the Dodo's population.

In addition to predation, habitat destruction also contributed to the Dodo's decline. The settlers cleared large areas of Mauritius' forests for agriculture, reducing the Dodo's feeding and nesting grounds. The combination of hunting, predation by introduced species, and habitat loss led to the Dodo's extinction within just a few decades of human arrival.

3. Modern Sightings and the Search for the Dodo
Despite its extinction over 300 years ago, stories of surviving Dodos have persisted, particularly in the folklore of Mauritius. Local legends speak of large, flightless birds that roam the island's forests, and occasional sightings of such birds have been reported by locals and tourists alike.

Early Reports of Surviving Dodos
In the early 19th century, several reports emerged of large, flightless birds being seen on Mauritius and nearby islands. These sightings were often dismissed as misidentifications of other birds, such as the Red Rail, a smaller flightless bird that also went extinct in the 1800s.

However, some reports were more compelling. In 1825, a French naturalist named Louis Bouton claimed to have seen a large, gray bird resembling the Dodo in the remote forests of Mauritius. Bouton's account was met with skepticism, but his description matched historical depictions of the Dodo.

Recent Sightings

In the 21st century, there have been occasional reports of large, flightless birds being seen in the less-explored areas of Mauritius. In 2009, a group of hikers claimed to have seen a bird resembling the Dodo near a waterfall in the Black River Gorges National Park. The hikers described the bird as being about 3 feet tall, with a large beak and a rounded body.

While no definitive evidence has been collected to support these sightings, they have sparked renewed interest in the possibility that a small population of Dodos, or a closely related species, might still exist in the region.

Fossil Discoveries and the Mystery of the Dodo

In recent years, fossil discoveries have provided new insights into the Dodo's biology and behavior. In 2005, a team of scientists excavating a cave on Mauritius discovered a treasure trove of Dodo bones, including several nearly complete skeletons. These fossils have allowed researchers to reconstruct the Dodo's anatomy in greater detail and have sparked interest in using DNA analysis to study the bird's evolutionary history.

Some researchers have suggested that the discovery of well-preserved Dodo DNA could pave the way for de-extinction efforts, similar to those being explored for other extinct species like the Woolly Mammoth. While the idea of bringing the Dodo back to life is still largely theoretical, it offers a tantalizing possibility for the future.

4. Could the Dodo Return?

The Dodo's extinction was one of the earliest examples of human-driven extinction, but modern science may offer a chance for redemption. Advances in genetic engineering and cloning technologies have opened up the possibility of bringing extinct species back to life, and the Dodo is often cited as a prime candidate for de-extinction.

Cloning and Genetic Engineering

To bring the Dodo back, scientists would need to obtain well-preserved Dodo DNA, which could then be inserted into the egg of a closely related species, such as the Nicobar pigeon. This process, known as somatic cell nuclear transfer, has been successfully used to clone other animals, but cloning an extinct species presents unique challenges.

One of the biggest obstacles to cloning the Dodo is the quality of the available DNA. While some well-preserved Dodo bones have been found, the DNA they contain is often fragmented and degraded. However, as DNA extraction techniques improve, it may become possible to recover enough genetic material to make cloning a reality.

The Ethics of De-Extinction

The idea of de-extincting the Dodo raises important ethical questions. Some conservationists argue that resources should be focused on protecting endangered species rather than bringing back extinct ones. Others worry that de-extinction could create ecological problems, as reintroduced species might disrupt modern ecosystems.

On the other hand, proponents of de-extinction argue that bringing back species like the Dodo could help restore ecosystems that have been altered by human activity. In the case of the Dodo, reintroducing the bird to Mauritius could help control invasive species and restore the island's native vegetation.

5. Conclusion: The Legacy of the Dodo

The Dodo's extinction has become a symbol of the fragility of island ecosystems and the devastating impact of human activity. While the bird is gone, its story continues to captivate the public imagination, and the possibility of its return through de-extinction offers hope for the future of conservation. Whether or not the Dodo can ever be brought back to life, its legacy serves as a reminder of the importance of protecting the world's remaining biodiversity.

THE QUAGGA: AFRICA'S EXTINCT ZEBRA WITH A MODERN TWIST

T he Quagga (Equus quagga quagga) was a unique subspecies of plains zebra, distinguished by its striking half-striped, half-brown coat. Once roaming the grasslands of South Africa in large herds, the Quagga was hunted to extinction by European settlers in the 19th century. However, recent efforts to revive the Quagga through selective breeding have raised the possibility that this extinct zebra might one day walk the Earth again.

In this chapter, we will explore the history of the Quagga, the reasons for its extinction, and the ambitious project known as the "Quagga Project," which aims to bring back this lost species through modern science.

1. The Quagga: A Zebra Like No Other

The Quagga was a unique zebra subspecies, characterized by its unusual coat pattern. Unlike other zebras, which have stripes covering their entire body, the Quagga had stripes only on the front half of its body, while its hindquarters were a solid brown color. This distinctive pattern made the Quagga one of the most recognizable animals in Africa.

Habitat and Behavior

Quaggas lived in the grasslands and savannas of South Africa, particularly in the Cape region. They were social animals, living in large herds that grazed on grasses and other vegetation. Like other zebras, Quaggas were highly adapted to life in open environments, relying on their speed and agility to escape predators such as lions and hyenas.

Quaggas were also known for their distinctive vocalizations, which were described as being more like the bark of a dog than the neigh of a horse. Their name, "Quagga," is thought to be derived from the sound of their call.

2. The Extinction of the Quagga

The Quagga was once widespread across the Cape region of South Africa, but its population began to decline rapidly in the 19th century due to overhunting and habitat loss.

Hunting and Habitat Loss

European settlers in South Africa hunted the Quagga extensively for its meat and hide. Quaggas were also killed to make room for livestock, as they competed with cattle and sheep for grazing land. By the mid-19th century, the Quagga population had been reduced to a few small herds, and the species was on the brink of extinction.

The last wild Quagga was killed in the late 1870s, and the last known Quagga, a female, died in captivity at the Amsterdam Zoo in 1883. With her death, the Quagga was officially declared extinct.

3. The Quagga Project: Bringing the Quagga Back to Life

In the 1980s, a South African researcher named Reinhold Rau launched an ambitious project to bring back the Quagga through selective breeding. Rau's idea was based on the fact that the Quagga was not a separate species, but rather a subspecies of the plains zebra. This meant that the genetic material needed to recreate the Quagga still existed in modern zebras.

Selective Breeding

The Quagga Project began by selecting plains zebras with the least amount of striping, similar to the Quagga's coat pattern. These zebras were then bred over several generations, with each generation producing offspring that more closely resembled the Quagga.

The goal of the project is to create a population of zebras that are visually indistinguishable from the original Quagga. While the animals produced by the project are not true Quaggas, as they lack the full genetic diversity of the original population, they are a close approximation of what the Quagga once looked like.

Successes and Challenges

The Quagga Project has seen some success, with several zebras now displaying coat patterns that closely resemble those of the Quagga. These animals have been released into protected reserves in South Africa, where they live and breed in semi-wild conditions.

However, the project has faced criticism from some conservationists, who argue that the animals produced by the project are not true Quaggas and that resources would be better spent on protecting existing endangered species. Others question whether the reintroduction of Quagga-like zebras could have unintended ecological consequences.

4. Could the Quagga Be Truly Resurrected?

While the Quagga Project has made significant strides in recreating the appearance of the Quagga, the question remains whether the Quagga could ever be truly resurrected. Advances in genetic engineering and cloning offer the possibility of reviving the Quagga using DNA from preserved specimens, but this technology is still in its early stages.

Cloning and Genetic Engineering

Several well-preserved Quagga skins exist in museums, and scientists have been able to extract DNA from these specimens. In theory, it may be possible to use this DNA to clone a Quagga, similar to the efforts being made to clone the Woolly Mammoth.

However, cloning an extinct animal presents numerous challenges, particularly when the species has been extinct for over a century. The quality of the DNA is often degraded, and the lack of genetic diversity in the surviving specimens makes it difficult to recreate a viable population.

5. Conclusion: The Quagga's Legacy

The story of the Quagga is a fascinating example of how modern science can be used to attempt to undo the damage of past human actions. While the Quagga Project has not yet fully resurrected the species, it has brought the Quagga back from the brink of oblivion, at least in appearance. The project also serves as a reminder of the importance of conservation and the need to protect the world's remaining biodiversity before more species are lost forever.

THE JAVAN TIGER: COULD IT STILL HAUNT THE JUNGLES?

T he Javan Tiger (Panthera tigris sondaica) was once a powerful predator that roamed the dense forests of the Indonesian island of Java. Despite its small size compared to other tigers, it was a fearsome hunter, well-adapted to the island's mountainous terrain and dense jungles. By the 1970s, however, the Javan Tiger was declared extinct due to habitat loss and hunting. Yet, like other vanished creatures, persistent reports and sightings suggest that this elusive tiger might still survive in the remote corners of Java.

This chapter will explore the biology of the Javan Tiger, the causes behind its extinction, the historical and cultural significance of tigers in Java, and the intriguing sightings and expeditions that continue to spark hope that this island predator may still roam the forests.

1. The Javan Tiger: A Small but Powerful Predator
The Javan Tiger was a small subspecies of tiger native to the Indonesian island of Java, one of the many subspecies of the *Panthera tigris* family that once roamed throughout Asia.

The Javan Tiger was similar to the now-extinct Bali Tiger and the critically endangered Sumatran Tiger, sharing both morphological and ecological traits.

Physical Characteristics

The Javan Tiger was among the smallest of the tiger subspecies, with males typically weighing between 220 to 310 pounds and females weighing around 170 to 240 pounds. These tigers measured around 6.5 to 8 feet in length, including their tail, and stood about 2.3 to 2.5 feet tall at the shoulder. Their smaller size made them well-suited to Java's rugged terrain and dense tropical forests, where agility was more important than brute strength.

The Javan Tiger's coat was deep orange, adorned with bold, closely spaced black stripes that helped it blend into the forest undergrowth. These stripes were narrower and more numerous than those of other tiger subspecies, giving the Javan Tiger a unique appearance.

Behavior and Ecology

Like all tigers, the Javan Tiger was a solitary and territorial animal. Its primary habitat was Java's dense rainforests and mountainous regions, where it could hunt a variety of prey, including deer, wild boar, and banteng (wild cattle). The Javan Tiger was a skilled hunter, using stealth and strength to ambush its prey. It would typically hunt at night or during the early morning hours when the forest was cooler and less crowded with human activity.

The Javan Tiger played a critical role in maintaining the balance of its ecosystem, serving as the apex predator of Java's forests. By controlling populations of herbivores like deer and boar, it helped prevent overgrazing and preserved the delicate balance of the island's vegetation.

2. Human Impact and the Path to Extinction

The Javan Tiger's decline was closely tied to human activity, beginning with Dutch colonization in the 17th century. As Java's population grew, vast areas of the island's forests were cleared to make way for agriculture, plantations, and settlements. This deforestation reduced the tiger's natural habitat, isolating populations and making it more difficult for them to find food.

Colonial Exploitation and Hunting

Java's colonial history played a significant role in the decline of its wildlife. During Dutch rule, the forests of Java were exploited for timber and agriculture. Large tracts of forest were converted into plantations for coffee, tea, and sugarcane, destroying much of the Javan Tiger's habitat. Additionally, European settlers and local aristocrats saw the Javan Tiger as both a pest and a trophy, leading to widespread hunting. Tigers were seen as a threat to livestock, and as such, tiger hunting became a common practice, with bounties offered for their capture or killing.

By the late 19th and early 20th centuries, tiger populations were in serious decline across Java. The Dutch colonial government began to impose hunting regulations, but these measures came too late to reverse the trend.

Habitat Destruction and Fragmentation

By the mid-20th century, Java's forests were under extreme pressure from deforestation. The island's burgeoning human population continued to expand into the remaining wilderness areas, further reducing the tiger's habitat. Deforestation not only reduced the tigers' territory but also fragmented their populations, isolating individuals and making it difficult for them to breed and maintain genetic diversity.

The construction of roads, railways, and infrastructure further fragmented the remaining tiger habitats, leading to increased human-wildlife conflict. Tigers were often killed in retaliation for livestock attacks, and their prey populations dwindled as human activity increased in their remaining strongholds.

Decline of Prey Species

As Java's forests were cleared for agriculture, many of the Javan Tiger's primary prey species, such as deer and wild boar, became scarce. This forced the tigers to either move into new territories or hunt livestock, which often resulted in deadly encounters with humans. The decline in prey availability placed additional stress on the Javan Tiger population, further accelerating its decline.

3. The Final Days of the Javan Tiger: Extinction or Survival?

By the mid-20th century, the Javan Tiger was on the brink of extinction. The last confirmed sightings of the Javan Tiger occurred in the 1970s, with the population estimated to be fewer than 20 individuals by that time. The Ujung Kulon National Park, located in the southwestern tip of Java, was one of the last known refuges for the species.

The Last Known Population

Ujung Kulon became the focus of conservation efforts to save the Javan Tiger in the 1950s and 1960s. However, by the 1970s, the population had dwindled to just a few individuals. The park, while offering some protection, was still vulnerable to illegal hunting and encroachment by local farmers. A lack of funding and resources hampered efforts to protect the remaining tigers.

The last confirmed sighting of the Javan Tiger occurred in 1976, when a forestry worker reported seeing a tiger in the Meru Betiri National Park on the eastern coast of Java. Despite this sighting, no further evidence of the Javan Tiger's survival has been found, and the species was officially declared extinct in the 1990s.

4. Modern Sightings and the Hope for Survival

Despite the official declaration of the Javan Tiger's extinction, reports of tiger sightings have continued to surface in Java. Many locals, particularly those living in remote forest areas, claim to have encountered tigers, describing animals that resemble the Javan Tiger in size, color, and behavior.

Eyewitness Reports
In the years following the tiger's official extinction, numerous reports of sightings emerged from local villagers, hunters, and forestry workers. Many of these reports came from Java's remaining national parks, particularly Meru Betiri and Ujung Kulon, where the last known populations were once found.

One of the most compelling sightings occurred in 1995 when park rangers in Meru Betiri discovered fresh tracks that they believed belonged to a tiger. The tracks were larger than those of leopards, the only other large cat species in Java, and showed characteristics consistent with tiger footprints. However, no photographic or physical evidence was collected at the time.

In 2008, an Indonesian conservationist working in the Gunung Halimun National Park reported hearing the distinctive roar of a tiger while conducting fieldwork. Although no visual confirmation was made, the roar was distinct enough to raise speculation that the Javan Tiger might still exist in the park's remote interior.

Camera Traps and Expeditions
Modern technology has been employed in the search for the Javan Tiger, particularly the use of camera traps. In the early 2000s, conservationists set up camera traps in Meru Betiri and Ujung Kulon to capture images of any surviving tigers. While the traps did capture images of leopards and other wildlife, no tigers were recorded.

In 2010, an expedition funded by the Indonesian government set out to search for evidence of surviving Javan Tigers. The team focused on areas where recent sightings had been reported, but after several months, the expedition yielded no conclusive evidence.

Explanations for the Sightings

While many sightings of the Javan Tiger have been reported over the years, the lack of concrete evidence has led to skepticism among scientists. Some researchers believe that the sightings could be misidentifications of leopards or other large animals. Javan leopards, which are still present on the island, have a more variable coat pattern than other leopard subspecies and can appear similar to tigers in low-light conditions.

Others suggest that the reports of tigers may be a combination of folklore and wishful thinking. The Javan Tiger holds a special place in the cultural history of Java, and the idea that the species could still survive resonates strongly with local communities.

5. The Cultural Significance of the Javan Tiger

The Javan Tiger has long been a symbol of strength, power, and mystery in Javanese culture. In traditional folklore, tigers are seen as protectors of the forest and are often associated with spiritual beliefs. Even today, stories of tiger spirits, known as "Macan Putih" or "white tigers," are still told by rural villagers in Java, who believe these spirits guard the forests and protect the land from harm.

Tigers in Folklore and Mythology

In Javanese mythology, tigers are often depicted as sacred animals, revered for their strength and bravery. Tigers are believed to have supernatural powers, and many legends tell of tigers that could transform into human beings or serve as guardians of royal families. These myths have helped cement the tiger's place as a symbol of leadership and protection in Javanese culture.

The Javan Tiger in Modern Culture

In modern Java, the Javan Tiger is remembered as a symbol of the island's once-thriving wilderness. The tiger's extinction is viewed as a tragic loss, both for the environment and for Javanese culture. However, the ongoing reports of sightings, along with the deep cultural connection to tigers, have kept the hope alive that the Javan Tiger might still exist in the island's remote forests.

6. Conclusion: The Elusive Javan Tiger

The Javan Tiger remains one of the most intriguing cryptozoological mysteries of Southeast Asia. While the official record states that the species is extinct, the persistent sightings and cultural significance of the tiger suggest that its story is not yet over. Whether the Javan Tiger still exists in the hidden jungles of Java or survives only in the memories and folklore of its people, it serves as a powerful reminder of the fragility of island ecosystems and the consequences of human impact.

THE PASSENGER PIGEON: CAN THE MOST ABUNDANT BIRD COME BACK?

The Passenger Pigeon (Ectopistes migratorius) was once the most abundant bird in North America, with flocks numbering in the billions. Their migrations were a spectacle, darkening the skies for hours or even days as they passed overhead. However, within just a few decades, relentless hunting and habitat destruction drove the species to extinction, with the last known Passenger Pigeon, named Martha, dying in captivity in 1914. Today, efforts to bring back the Passenger Pigeon through de-extinction are underway, raising hopes that this iconic bird might one day return to the skies.

In this chapter, we will explore the biology of the Passenger Pigeon, the factors behind its rapid extinction, and the ambitious efforts to revive the species using modern science.

1. The Passenger Pigeon: A Bird of the Skies

Passenger Pigeons were medium-sized birds, closely related to the Mourning Dove. They were characterized by their slender bodies, long tails, and iridescent plumage, which ranged from reddish-bronze to gray-blue, depending on the bird's age and sex.

Physical Characteristics and Behavior

Passenger Pigeons were highly social birds, living in massive flocks that could number in the billions. They were fast and agile flyers, capable of reaching speeds of up to 60 miles per hour. Their name, "Passenger Pigeon," comes from the French word *passager*, meaning "passing by," a reference to their migratory behavior.

These pigeons were nomadic, traveling great distances in search of food and suitable nesting sites. They primarily fed on mast —acorns, beech nuts, and chestnuts—which they consumed in large quantities. Their migration patterns were closely tied to the availability of these food sources, and they would often travel hundreds of miles in a single day to find new feeding grounds.

Passenger Pigeons were known for their communal nesting behavior, with thousands of birds nesting in a single tree. These massive nesting colonies, known as "pigeon cities," could cover several square miles, with millions of birds raising their young in close proximity. The sheer size of these colonies made them a dominant force in the ecosystems they inhabited, influencing the growth and distribution of plant species and providing food for predators.

2. The Rise and Fall of the Passenger Pigeon

The rapid extinction of the Passenger Pigeon is one of the most dramatic and tragic examples of human impact on wildlife. In the early 19th century, the Passenger Pigeon was the most abundant bird in North America, with a population estimated at 3 to 5 billion. However, within just a few decades, overhunting and habitat destruction led to the species' near-total collapse.

Hunting and Commercial Exploitation

The abundance of Passenger Pigeons made them a valuable target for hunters. In the 19th century, the commercial hunting of pigeons became a booming industry. The birds were shot by the thousands, often using nets, traps, and firearms, and their meat was sold in markets across the United States.

Passenger Pigeons were particularly vulnerable to overhunting due to their communal behavior. Hunters would locate nesting colonies and kill thousands of birds in a single day, often leaving the young to starve. The birds' fast flight made them challenging targets, but the sheer number of pigeons ensured that hunters could still kill vast numbers.

The development of railroads and telegraph networks in the mid-19th century allowed hunters to track the movements of pigeon flocks more efficiently, further accelerating the slaughter. As the birds' populations declined, hunting intensified, with some hunters even resorting to using dynamite to kill large numbers of pigeons at once.

Habitat Loss and Deforestation
In addition to hunting, habitat loss played a significant role in the decline of the Passenger Pigeon. The expansion of agriculture and logging in the eastern United States led to widespread deforestation, reducing the availability of the mast that the pigeons relied on for food.

The loss of large tracts of forest also disrupted the pigeons' nesting behavior. Without access to the vast, undisturbed forests they needed for communal nesting, the pigeons were forced into smaller, more fragmented habitats, making them even more vulnerable to hunting and predation.

The Final Days of the Passenger Pigeon
By the late 19th century, the Passenger Pigeon population had been reduced to just a few thousand individuals. The last large-scale nesting colony was reported in Michigan in 1878, and by the 1890s, sightings of wild Passenger Pigeons were rare.

The last confirmed wild Passenger Pigeon was shot in Ohio in 1900. After that, only a few individuals remained in captivity, including Martha, the last known Passenger Pigeon, who lived at the Cincinnati Zoo. Martha died on September 1, 1914, marking the official extinction of the species.

3. De-Extinction: Could the Passenger Pigeon Return?

The extinction of the Passenger Pigeon was a wake-up call for conservationists, highlighting the devastating impact of unchecked exploitation and habitat destruction. Today, the Passenger Pigeon has become a symbol of de-extinction, the process of using genetic engineering to bring back extinct species.

The Science of De-Extinction

De-extinction efforts for the Passenger Pigeon are being led by a group of scientists and conservationists, including the organization Revive & Restore. The goal of the project is to recreate a living Passenger Pigeon using modern genetic engineering techniques.

The first step in the de-extinction process is to sequence the Passenger Pigeon's genome. Fortunately, several well-preserved Passenger Pigeon specimens exist in museums, and scientists have successfully extracted DNA from these specimens. By comparing the Passenger Pigeon's genome with that of its closest living relative, the Band-tailed Pigeon, researchers can identify the specific genes that made the Passenger Pigeon unique.

Once the Passenger Pigeon's genome has been sequenced, the next step is to use CRISPR gene-editing technology to insert the Passenger Pigeon's genes into the DNA of Band-tailed Pigeon embryos. These embryos would then be implanted into surrogate pigeons, which would give birth to chicks that are genetically similar to Passenger Pigeons.

Challenges and Ethical Considerations

While the science of de-extinction is promising, there are several challenges and ethical concerns associated with bringing the Passenger Pigeon back to life. One of the biggest challenges is ensuring that the recreated Passenger Pigeons are capable of surviving in modern ecosystems. The forests that once supported billions of pigeons have been drastically altered by human activity, and it is unclear whether the pigeons could thrive in their old habitats.

There are also ethical questions about whether de-extinction is the best use of conservation resources. Some critics argue that efforts should be focused on protecting existing endangered species rather than bringing back extinct ones. Others worry that de-extinct species could disrupt modern ecosystems or become invasive.

Despite these challenges, proponents of de-extinction argue that bringing back the Passenger Pigeon could help restore some of the ecological functions that were lost when the species went extinct. For example, Passenger Pigeons played a crucial role in shaping the forests of North America, and their reintroduction could help regenerate forest ecosystems.

4. The Ecological Importance of the Passenger Pigeon

The extinction of the Passenger Pigeon had a profound impact on the ecosystems of eastern North America. As one of the most abundant birds in the region, Passenger Pigeons played a key role in shaping the structure and composition of forests.

Seed Dispersal and Forest Regeneration

Passenger Pigeons were important seed dispersers, particularly for mast-producing trees such as oaks, beeches, and chestnuts. The pigeons would consume large quantities of seeds and then excrete them in new locations, helping to spread trees across the landscape.

The loss of the Passenger Pigeon likely contributed to changes in the composition of North American forests. Without the pigeons to disperse seeds, certain tree species may have become less common, while others, such as maples, may have become more dominant.

Nutrient Cycling

The sheer number of Passenger Pigeons also played a role in nutrient cycling within forests. The pigeons' droppings, or guano, provided a rich source of nutrients for plants and helped fertilize the soil. In areas where large nesting colonies were established, the accumulation of guano would have had significant effects on soil fertility and plant growth.

Food for Predators

Passenger Pigeons were a major food source for a variety of predators, including hawks, eagles, foxes, and even humans. The sudden loss of such a large and abundant food source would have had ripple effects throughout the food chain, forcing predators to shift their diets to other species.

5. Conclusion: The Legacy of the Passenger Pigeon

The Passenger Pigeon's extinction serves as a powerful reminder of the fragility of nature and the devastating consequences of human exploitation. While the species is gone, its legacy lives on in the efforts to bring it back through de-extinction and in the lessons it has taught us about the need for conservation.

The idea of Passenger Pigeons once again filling the skies of North America is both exciting and sobering. Whether or not the species can be successfully revived, the story of the Passenger Pigeon remains one of the most important cautionary tales in the history of conservation.

THE PLEISTOCENE CAVE LION: A KING OF THE ICE AGE

The Pleistocene Cave Lion (Panthera leo spelaea), also known as the European Cave Lion, was one of the largest and most formidable predators of the Ice Age. Roaming across Europe and northern Asia, these lions were larger and more robust than their modern counterparts, preying on a wide variety of Ice Age megafauna. Despite their impressive size and strength, Cave Lions went extinct around 12,000 years ago, possibly due to climate change and competition with humans.

However, recent discoveries of remarkably well-preserved Cave Lion cubs in Siberia have sparked interest in the possibility of reviving the species through cloning. In this chapter, we will explore the biology of the Pleistocene Cave Lion, the factors behind its extinction, and the scientific efforts to bring this ancient predator back to life.

1. The Pleistocene Cave Lion: An Apex Predator

The Pleistocene Cave Lion was a subspecies of the modern lion, but it was larger and more robust, with some individuals weighing up to 880 pounds—nearly twice the size of modern

African lions. Cave Lions were well-adapted to the harsh conditions of the Ice Age, with a muscular build and thick fur to protect them from the cold.

Physical Characteristics

Cave Lions were similar in appearance to modern lions, but they were larger and more powerfully built. Males may have had less prominent manes, or no manes at all, which would have made them more similar in appearance to modern lionesses. This lack of a mane would have reduced the risk of frostbite in the cold climates where they lived.

Cave Lions had long, powerful legs, which allowed them to run at high speeds to catch prey. Their massive paws were equipped with sharp claws, which they used to bring down large animals. The Cave Lion's teeth were also formidable, with long, sharp canines designed for piercing the flesh of its prey.

Behavior and Hunting

Cave Lions were apex predators, sitting at the top of the Ice Age food chain. They preyed on a wide variety of animals, including reindeer, horses, bison, and even mammoths. Cave paintings from the Upper Paleolithic period depict Cave Lions hunting in groups, suggesting that they may have been social animals, like modern lions.

The Cave Lion's habitat included the cold, open plains of Europe, northern Asia, and Alaska, where it would have hunted in packs to take down large prey. Some scientists believe that Cave Lions may have also scavenged from the kills of other predators, such as wolves and hyenas, but they were primarily hunters.

2. Extinction: Climate Change and Human Impact

The extinction of the Pleistocene Cave Lion coincided with the end of the last Ice Age, a period of significant climate change that caused the disappearance of many large mammal species, known as the megafauna. The exact reasons for the Cave Lion's extinction are still debated, but several factors likely contributed.

Climate Change and Habitat Loss

As the Ice Age came to an end, the Earth's climate warmed, causing glaciers to retreat and altering the landscapes where Cave Lions lived. The open grasslands and tundra that the lions depended on for hunting gradually disappeared, replaced by forests that were less suitable for large predators.

The warming climate also affected the populations of the Cave Lion's prey. Many of the large herbivores that Cave Lions relied on for food, such as mammoths and woolly rhinoceroses, went extinct or migrated to new regions. As their prey disappeared, Cave Lions would have struggled to find enough food to survive.

Competition with Humans

The arrival of humans in Europe and northern Asia during the Upper Paleolithic period may have also played a role in the Cave Lion's extinction. Early humans were skilled hunters who competed with Cave Lions for prey. They may have also hunted Cave Lions directly, as lion skins would have provided valuable warmth during the cold Ice Age winters.

There is evidence that humans and Cave Lions occasionally clashed, as suggested by the discovery of lion bones in human settlements and the depiction of lions in ancient cave art. Some researchers believe that humans may have intentionally killed Cave Lions to reduce competition for food.

3. Recent Discoveries: Frozen Cave Lions in Siberia

In recent years, the discovery of remarkably well-preserved Cave Lion cubs in the permafrost of Siberia has provided new insights into the biology of these ancient predators. These frozen cubs, which are estimated to be around 30,000 years old, are among the best-preserved Ice Age animals ever found.

The Discovery of the Cave Lion Cubs

In 2015, a team of Russian scientists discovered two frozen Cave Lion cubs in the Siberian permafrost. The cubs, nicknamed "Uyan" and "Dina," were in an astonishing state of preservation, with their fur, whiskers, and even internal organs intact. The cubs were estimated to be around one to two months old when they died, and they likely perished when their den collapsed.

The discovery of Uyan and Dina was followed by the discovery of two more Cave Lion cubs in 2017, found in the same region of Siberia. These cubs, nicknamed "Boris" and "Sparta," were even better preserved than the first pair, with fully intact fur and muscle tissue.

Insights from the Frozen Cubs

The frozen cubs have provided scientists with a wealth of information about the biology and behavior of Cave Lions. The cubs' thick fur suggests that Cave Lions were well-adapted to the cold climates of the Ice Age, and their muscular build indicates that they were powerful animals from a young age.

Researchers have also been able to extract DNA from the cubs, which has provided new insights into the genetic differences between Cave Lions and modern lions. These genetic studies have confirmed that Cave Lions were a distinct subspecies, though they were closely related to modern lions and could potentially be brought back through cloning.

4. Cloning the Cave Lion: The Possibility of De-Extinction

The discovery of well-preserved Cave Lion cubs has sparked interest in the possibility of bringing the species back to life through cloning. Advances in genetic engineering and cloning technology have made it theoretically possible to revive extinct species, and the Cave Lion is seen as a prime candidate for de-extinction.

The Science of Cloning

To clone a Cave Lion, scientists would need to extract viable DNA from the frozen cubs and insert it into the egg of a closely related species, such as a modern lion or a tiger. The egg would then be implanted into a surrogate mother, which would give birth to a cloned Cave Lion cub.

While the science of cloning has advanced significantly in recent years, there are still many challenges associated with cloning extinct species. One of the biggest challenges is obtaining high-quality DNA from the frozen cubs, as much of the DNA is degraded after thousands of years. However, researchers are optimistic that improvements in DNA sequencing and editing technologies will make cloning a reality in the near future.

Ethical and Ecological Considerations

The possibility of cloning the Cave Lion raises several ethical and ecological questions. One of the main concerns is whether it is appropriate to bring back a species that has been extinct for thousands of years. Some conservationists argue that resources should be focused on protecting existing endangered species rather than reviving extinct ones.

There are also concerns about the ecological impact of reintroducing Cave Lions into the wild. The ecosystems that Cave Lions once inhabited have changed significantly since the Ice Age, and it is unclear whether modern ecosystems could support such a large predator.

5. Conclusion: The Legacy of the Cave Lion

The Pleistocene Cave Lion was one of the most formidable predators of the Ice Age, and its extinction marked the end of an era in which large predators dominated the landscape. While the species is gone, recent discoveries of frozen cubs have brought the Cave Lion back into the spotlight, raising the possibility that this ancient predator could one day be revived.

The story of the Cave Lion is a reminder of the fragility of life in the face of changing climates and human impact. Whether or not the species is ever brought back to life, its legacy will continue to inspire scientific exploration and a deeper understanding of the world's ancient past.

THE STELLER'S SEA COW: A MARINE GIANT LOST TO TIME

The Steller's Sea Cow (Hydrodamalis gigas) was a massive marine mammal that once inhabited the cold waters of the North Pacific. Measuring up to 30 feet in length and weighing as much as 10 tons, these gentle giants were relatives of the modern-day dugong and manatee. Sadly, within just 27 years of being discovered by European explorers, the Steller's Sea Cow was hunted to extinction.

Despite its official extinction in the 18th century, some cryptozoologists and local fishermen have reported sightings of large, unidentified marine creatures in the same waters once inhabited by the sea cow. Could it be that this giant of the sea still survives, hidden in the depths of the North Pacific?

1. The Steller's Sea Cow: A Gentle Giant of the North Pacific
The Steller's Sea Cow was one of the largest marine mammals ever recorded, rivaling whales in size. It was a slow-moving, herbivorous animal that lived in shallow coastal waters, where it fed on kelp and other marine vegetation.

Physical Characteristics

Steller's Sea Cows were massive, with adults reaching lengths of 25 to 30 feet and weighing between 8 to 10 tons. Their bodies were long and cylindrical, with thick, blubber-covered skin that helped insulate them from the cold waters of the North Pacific. Unlike their modern relatives, such as the dugong and manatee, Steller's Sea Cows had no dorsal fin and a flattened tail, which they used to propel themselves through the water.

Their heads were small in proportion to their bodies, with broad, flat snouts that they used to graze on kelp beds. Steller's Sea Cows had large, paddle-like forelimbs that they used to maneuver in shallow waters and forage for food.

Habitat and Diet

Steller's Sea Cows lived in the cold, shallow waters of the Bering Sea, particularly around the Commander Islands off the coast of Russia. They were highly specialized herbivores, feeding exclusively on kelp and other marine vegetation. Their slow metabolism and large size allowed them to subsist on relatively small amounts of food, but they needed access to vast kelp beds to sustain their populations.

These gentle giants spent most of their time grazing on kelp, using their forelimbs to anchor themselves to rocks while they fed. Their slow movements and peaceful nature made them easy targets for predators, including humans.

2. The Discovery and Rapid Extinction of the Steller's Sea Cow

The Steller's Sea Cow was first described by the German naturalist Georg Wilhelm Steller in 1741, during an expedition led by the Russian explorer Vitus Bering. Steller's account of the sea cow provides the only detailed description of the species, as it was hunted to extinction within a few decades of its discovery.

Steller's Account

In his writings, Steller described the sea cows as gentle and docile creatures, often seen in small groups near the shore. He noted their slow movements and lack of fear of humans, which made them easy prey for hunters. Steller also observed that the sea cows were social animals, often seen interacting with one another and showing signs of affection.

Steller's Sea Cows were hunted for their meat, blubber, and hide. Their blubber was particularly valuable, as it was thick and could be rendered into oil for lamps. Their hides were used to make boats and other durable goods, while their meat provided a source of food for sailors and settlers in the harsh environments of the North Pacific.

Hunting and Extinction
The discovery of the Steller's Sea Cow coincided with the rise of Russian fur traders in the North Pacific, who hunted the animals relentlessly for their valuable resources. The sea cows, already vulnerable due to their slow reproduction rates and limited range, were unable to withstand the pressures of hunting.

By 1768, just 27 years after their discovery, the last known Steller's Sea Cow was killed by hunters. The species was officially declared extinct, marking one of the fastest extinctions in recorded history.

3. Could Steller's Sea Cows Still Survive?
Despite their official extinction, there have been occasional reports of large, unidentified marine animals being sighted in the waters of the Bering Sea and the Commander Islands. These reports have sparked speculation that a small population of Steller's Sea Cows may still exist in the remote, unexplored regions of the North Pacific.

Eyewitness Reports
Fishermen and sailors in the Bering Sea have occasionally

reported sightings of large, slow-moving marine creatures that resemble descriptions of the Steller's Sea Cow. These creatures are often described as being much larger than modern-day dugongs or manatees, with broad, flat tails and smooth, blubber-covered skin.

One of the most well-known reports comes from 1962 when a group of Russian fishermen claimed to have seen a massive sea creature near the Commander Islands. The fishermen described the creature as being over 20 feet long, with a large, rounded body and a flat tail. While no photographs or physical evidence were collected, the sighting fueled speculation that Steller's Sea Cows might still survive in the remote waters of the North Pacific.

Scientific Skepticism

Most scientists are skeptical of the idea that Steller's Sea Cows could still exist, citing the lack of physical evidence and the species' limited reproductive capacity. The sea cows had a slow reproductive rate, with females giving birth to only one calf every few years. This, combined with their small range and vulnerability to hunting, makes it unlikely that they could have survived undetected for over two centuries.

Additionally, the shallow coastal waters where the sea cows once lived are now heavily trafficked by ships and fishing boats, making it difficult for a large, slow-moving animal to remain hidden.

4. The Ecological Impact of the Steller's Sea Cow's Extinction

The extinction of the Steller's Sea Cow had a significant impact on the ecosystems of the North Pacific, particularly on the kelp forests where the sea cows once lived. As herbivores, Steller's Sea Cows played a crucial role in maintaining the health of kelp forests by controlling the growth of kelp and preventing it from becoming overgrown.

Kelp Forest Ecosystems

Kelp forests are some of the most productive and biodiverse

ecosystems in the world, providing habitat and food for a wide variety of marine species. Steller's Sea Cows helped maintain the balance of these ecosystems by grazing on kelp and preventing it from growing too densely. Their feeding behavior also helped create open spaces within kelp forests, which allowed sunlight to reach the ocean floor and supported the growth of other marine plants.

The loss of the Steller's Sea Cow likely contributed to changes in the structure of kelp forests in the Bering Sea. Without the sea cows to control kelp growth, some areas may have experienced overgrowth, which can lead to a decline in biodiversity and the health of the ecosystem.

Interactions with Other Marine Species

Steller's Sea Cows were part of a complex marine ecosystem that included sea otters, fish, and invertebrates. Sea otters, in particular, played a key role in maintaining the health of kelp forests by preying on sea urchins, which feed on kelp. The extinction of the sea cow may have shifted the balance of this ecosystem, as other species had to adapt to the loss of such a large herbivore.

5. Conclusion: The Lost Giant of the Sea

The extinction of the Steller's Sea Cow is a poignant reminder of the fragility of marine ecosystems and the devastating impact of overhunting. While the species is officially extinct, the occasional reports of large, unidentified marine creatures in the Bering Sea keep the possibility of its survival alive in the minds of cryptozoologists and local fishermen.

Whether or not the Steller's Sea Cow still exists, its story serves as a cautionary tale about the importance of conserving the world's remaining marine species and protecting the delicate balance of ocean ecosystems. The loss of this gentle giant continues to resonate as one of the most rapid and tragic extinctions in history.

THE KING ISLAND EMU: AUSTRALIA'S SMALLEST EMU, GONE OR SURVIVING?

The King Island Emu (Dromaius ater) was one of the smallest emu subspecies ever known, inhabiting King Island, which lies in the Bass Strait between mainland Australia and Tasmania. Much smaller than the modern-day emu, the King Island Emu was hunted to extinction in the early 19th century after European settlers arrived on the island. However, rumors and possible sightings have occasionally surfaced, leading to speculation that this diminutive emu could still survive in isolated regions.

In this chapter, we'll dive into the biology of the King Island Emu, its role in the island's ecosystem, the factors leading to its extinction, and the persistent whispers suggesting that this small emu may still wander the wilds of King Island.

1. The King Island Emu: A Miniature Emu of Australia

The King Island Emu was a distinct subspecies of emu, closely related to its much larger mainland cousin, the Australian Emu (*Dromaius novaehollandiae*). It is believed that the emu population on King Island became isolated from the mainland after rising sea levels at the end of the last Ice Age.

Physical Characteristics
The King Island Emu was much smaller than its mainland counterpart, standing at around 4 to 5 feet tall, compared to the modern emu's height of 6 feet. This smaller size was likely an adaptation to the limited resources available on the island. It weighed approximately 25 to 50 pounds, compared to the 100 to 130 pounds of the mainland emu.

Its feathers were similar to those of the Australian Emu, consisting of soft, downy plumage that helped regulate its body temperature in the cool climate of King Island. The emu had long, slender legs adapted for running, and although it was flightless like all emu species, it was a fast runner, capable of sprinting away from predators or human hunters.

Ecology and Behavior
Like other emus, the King Island Emu was primarily a herbivore, feeding on a variety of plant matter, including seeds, fruits, leaves, and grasses. It also played a critical role in seed dispersal, as many plants on the island relied on the emu to help spread their seeds across the landscape.

The emus were known to travel in small groups, and during breeding season, pairs would establish territories. The male emu was responsible for incubating the eggs and caring for the chicks after they hatched, a trait common to all emu species.

2. The Arrival of Humans and the Path to Extinction
The extinction of the King Island Emu was driven largely by human activities, particularly after European settlers arrived on King Island in the early 19th century. The island was initially used as a stopover for whalers and sealers, but by the early 1800s, settlers began to establish permanent farms on the island.

Impact of European Settlement

As settlers began to farm and clear land, the natural habitat of the King Island Emu was quickly destroyed. Forests were cleared for agriculture, and the emu's food sources became increasingly scarce. The settlers, unfamiliar with the wildlife of the region, also began hunting the emus for their meat and feathers.

By the time Europeans arrived, the emu population was already relatively small due to the island's limited carrying capacity. This made the species particularly vulnerable to overhunting and habitat destruction. The arrival of domesticated animals such as sheep and cattle further displaced the emus from their natural feeding grounds.

Overhunting and Exploitation

The King Island Emu was also hunted by whalers and sealers who visited the island. These hunters saw the emu as a source of fresh meat and feathers, which were prized for bedding and clothing. In some cases, emus were captured and taken aboard ships to provide a steady food supply for sailors during long voyages.

Unlike mainland Australia, where emus were widespread, the King Island Emu had no vast interior to escape into. As a result, the small emu population was quickly decimated. By 1822, just a few years after permanent settlement began, the King Island Emu was declared extinct in the wild.

The Extinction of Other Emu Subspecies

The King Island Emu was not the only emu subspecies to face extinction. Other island subspecies, such as the Kangaroo Island Emu (*Dromaius baudinianus*) and the Tasmanian Emu (*Dromaius diemenensis*), also went extinct due to similar pressures from human settlement and hunting. These smaller island populations were particularly vulnerable to extinction because of their limited genetic diversity and small population sizes.

3. Modern Sightings and Speculation on Survival

Despite the official declaration of extinction, occasional reports of emu-like birds on King Island have surfaced over the years, sparking speculation that the King Island Emu might still survive in some remote areas of the island.

Eyewitness Accounts

In the early 20th century, a few local farmers and travelers reported seeing large, flightless birds resembling emus in the more isolated parts of King Island. These sightings were often brief and occurred in the dense bushland, where the birds could easily disappear into the undergrowth. Some of these reports were dismissed as misidentifications of large, wild birds such as turkeys or introduced ostriches.

One of the more compelling sightings occurred in the 1940s, when a group of hunters claimed to have seen a small group of emu-like birds while traveling through the western part of the island. The hunters described the birds as smaller than mainland emus, with shorter legs and dark plumage—characteristics consistent with the King Island Emu.

Searches and Expeditions

Over the years, several expeditions have been launched to search for surviving populations of the King Island Emu, but none have been successful in providing conclusive evidence. In the 1970s, a group of ornithologists from Australia visited the island to investigate claims of emu sightings. The team set up camera traps and conducted interviews with locals, but no physical evidence was found.

Modern technology, such as drone surveys and satellite imaging, could potentially aid in future searches for surviving emus, but the dense and rugged terrain of King Island makes such efforts challenging. Furthermore, the lack of confirmed sightings in recent decades has led many scientists to believe that the species is truly extinct.

4. The Role of the King Island Emu in the Ecosystem

The extinction of the King Island Emu had a significant impact on the island's ecosystem. As a primary seed disperser and herbivore, the emu played a critical role in maintaining the balance of plant species on the island. Its grazing and seed dispersal activities helped shape the island's vegetation patterns, preventing the overgrowth of certain plant species and promoting biodiversity.

Changes in Vegetation

With the loss of the King Island Emu, certain plant species that relied on the bird for seed dispersal began to decline. These plants, many of which produced large seeds or fruits, were no longer able to spread their seeds as effectively, leading to changes in the composition of the island's vegetation.

The emu's absence also allowed other herbivores, such as introduced sheep and cattle, to dominate the landscape. These animals had different feeding habits and often overgrazed the land, leading to soil erosion and the decline of native plant species. The loss of the emu's ecological role contributed to the long-term degradation of King Island's natural environment.

Potential Ecological Impact of Reintroduction

If the King Island Emu were to be reintroduced—either through a rediscovered population or through de-extinction efforts—it could potentially help restore the island's degraded ecosystems. By reintroducing the emu's grazing and seed-dispersing behaviors, conservationists could promote the regeneration of native plant species and improve the overall health of the island's ecosystems.

However, such a reintroduction would need to be carefully managed, as the island's environment has changed significantly since the emu's extinction. New challenges, such as invasive species and habitat fragmentation, would need to be addressed to ensure the emu's survival in a modern context.

5. Could the King Island Emu Be Resurrected?

The King Island Emu, like several other extinct species, has been proposed as a candidate for de-extinction efforts. Advances in genetic engineering and cloning technology have raised the possibility of recreating the King Island Emu using DNA extracted from preserved specimens.

De-Extinction Efforts

Several well-preserved King Island Emu specimens exist in museum collections, including feathers, bones, and eggs. Using these samples, scientists could potentially extract DNA and use CRISPR gene-editing technology to recreate a genetically similar bird. By comparing the DNA of the King Island Emu to that of the mainland emu, researchers could identify the specific genes responsible for the island emu's smaller size and unique traits.

The reintroduction of a genetically engineered King Island Emu would raise several ethical and ecological questions. While it could potentially help restore the island's ecosystems, it would also require careful management to prevent unintended consequences, such as competition with other species or the spread of disease.

Conservation Priorities

As with other de-extinction efforts, some conservationists argue that resources would be better spent protecting existing endangered species rather than bringing back extinct ones. While the idea of resurrecting the King Island Emu is scientifically exciting, the practical challenges of reintroducing the species into a dramatically altered environment may outweigh the potential benefits.

6. Conclusion: The Legacy of the King Island Emu

The King Island Emu's extinction serves as a powerful reminder of the fragility of island ecosystems and the devastating impact of human colonization. While the species is officially extinct, the occasional reports of emu-like birds and the possibility of de-extinction keep the memory of this small, unique bird alive.

Whether or not the King Island Emu is ever rediscovered or resurrected, its story highlights the importance of protecting the world's remaining biodiversity and ensuring that future generations do not have to bear witness to more extinctions.

THE HAAST'S EAGLE: GIANT BIRD OF PREY OR MYTHIC HUNTER?

The Haast's Eagle (Harpagornis moorei) was the largest eagle to ever live, dominating the skies over New Zealand until it went extinct around 600 years ago. Known for its immense size and powerful hunting abilities, the Haast's Eagle preyed on the flightless Moa, another extinct giant bird of New Zealand. Despite its extinction, the Haast's Eagle has captured the imagination of cryptozoologists and bird enthusiasts, and occasional reports of large, unidentified birds in remote parts of New Zealand have sparked speculation that this apex predator might still exist.

In this chapter, we'll explore the biology of the Haast's Eagle, its role in New Zealand's ecosystems, the reasons for its extinction, and the possibility that this giant bird of prey could still be alive in the rugged wilderness of New Zealand.

1. The Haast's Eagle: The Largest Eagle to Ever Soar

The Haast's Eagle was a massive bird of prey, with a wingspan of up to 10 feet and a body length of nearly 5 feet. It was twice the size of the largest modern eagles, such as the Harpy Eagle, and weighed between 25 and 35 pounds—an enormous weight for a flying bird. The Haast's Eagle was perfectly adapted to hunt the giant Moa, which were flightless birds weighing up to 500 pounds.

Physical Characteristics
The Haast's Eagle had powerful talons, each as large as a tiger's claws, and a beak that could tear through flesh with ease. Its legs and feet were extremely strong, allowing it to grasp and immobilize its prey. The eagle's flight feathers were broad and long, enabling it to soar through the dense forests and mountainous regions of New Zealand in search of food.

Unlike many modern birds of prey, the Haast's Eagle was built for power rather than speed. It relied on its immense strength to overpower prey much larger than itself, using surprise attacks from above to kill its quarry. The eagle's hunting technique involved ambushing its prey, often from a perch high in the trees, before delivering a crushing blow with its talons.

Ecology and Behavior
The Haast's Eagle lived primarily in New Zealand's South Island, where it preyed on large herbivorous birds like the Moa. The eagle's diet was almost exclusively made up of Moa species, which varied in size but provided ample food for the giant bird of prey.

As the top predator in New Zealand's ecosystem, the Haast's Eagle had no natural enemies. Its dominance over the island's bird populations helped maintain the balance of the ecosystem by controlling the population of herbivores. The eagle's role in New Zealand's ecosystems was similar to that of large mammalian predators like lions and tigers in other parts of the world.

2. The Decline and Extinction of the Haast's Eagle
The extinction of the Haast's Eagle is closely tied to the extinction of its primary food source, the Moa. As with many of New Zealand's extinct species, the arrival of humans in the region led to

the rapid decline of the eagle and its prey.

Maori Arrival and the Decline of the Moa

The Maori people arrived in New Zealand around 1300 AD, bringing with them new hunting techniques and tools. The flightless Moa, which had no natural predators other than the Haast's Eagle, were easy targets for human hunters. The Maori hunted the Moa for their meat, feathers, and bones, and within a few centuries, the Moa population had been decimated.

As the Moa disappeared, so too did the Haast's Eagle's primary food source. Unable to find enough prey to sustain its population, the eagle's numbers began to decline. By the early 15th century, both the Moa and the Haast's Eagle had gone extinct, victims of human overhunting and habitat destruction.

Habitat Loss and Human Impact

In addition to hunting, the Maori cleared large areas of New Zealand's forests for agriculture and settlements. This deforestation reduced the eagle's hunting grounds and further contributed to its decline. The loss of forest cover made it difficult for the eagle to find suitable nesting sites and prey, accelerating its extinction.

While the Haast's Eagle was not directly hunted by humans, its reliance on the Moa for food and its need for large tracts of forested habitat made it highly vulnerable to the changes brought by human settlement.

3. Cryptozoology and Reports of Large Birds in New Zealand

Despite the Haast's Eagle's official extinction, occasional reports of large, unidentified birds have surfaced in New Zealand's remote regions. These reports have sparked speculation that the Haast's Eagle might still exist in isolated pockets of the South Island.

Eyewitness Accounts and Local Legends

In the 19th and early 20th centuries, several reports emerged of large birds being seen in New Zealand's South Island. Some of these sightings came from farmers and hunters who described seeing eagles much larger than any known living species. These birds were often described as having a massive wingspan and powerful talons, characteristics consistent with the Haast's Eagle. Local Maori legends also tell of giant birds known as "Pouakai" or "Hokioi," which were said to be large enough to carry off humans. While these legends are likely based on the Haast's Eagle, which would have been capable of killing a person, they have been passed down through generations, keeping the memory of the eagle alive in Maori culture.

Searches and Expeditions
Several expeditions have been launched to search for evidence of surviving Haast's Eagles, particularly in the remote forests of New Zealand's Fiordland region. However, no physical evidence has been found to support these claims, and most scientists remain skeptical of the idea that such a large bird could have survived unnoticed for centuries.

The rugged and isolated nature of New Zealand's South Island does offer some hope to cryptozoologists who believe that a small population of Haast's Eagles could still exist. The region's dense forests and mountainous terrain are difficult to explore, and much of the area remains relatively untouched by human activity.

4. Could the Haast's Eagle Be Revived?
Like other extinct species, the Haast's Eagle has been proposed as a candidate for de-extinction. Advances in genetic engineering and cloning could potentially allow scientists to bring the giant eagle back to life, using preserved DNA from fossilized remains.

De-Extinction Possibilities
Several well-preserved Haast's Eagle fossils have been discovered in New Zealand, providing scientists with a wealth of information

about the bird's anatomy and behavior. By extracting DNA from these fossils, researchers could potentially use CRISPR gene-editing technology to recreate a genetically similar eagle.

The reintroduction of a cloned Haast's Eagle would present several ecological and ethical challenges. The bird's primary food source, the Moa, is extinct, meaning that a revived Haast's Eagle would need to adapt to a new diet. Additionally, New Zealand's ecosystems have changed significantly since the eagle's extinction, and reintroducing such a large predator could disrupt modern ecosystems.

Conservation Priorities
As with other de-extinction efforts, some conservationists argue that resources should be focused on protecting existing endangered species rather than bringing back extinct ones. While the Haast's Eagle was a formidable predator, its role in New Zealand's ecosystems has already been replaced by other species, and the reintroduction of such a large predator could have unintended consequences.

5. The Cultural and Ecological Legacy of the Haast's Eagle
The Haast's Eagle's extinction marked the end of an era in New Zealand's natural history. As the largest eagle to ever live, the Haast's Eagle was a symbol of the island's unique wildlife and its ancient ecosystems.

Ecological Impact of the Eagle's Extinction
The extinction of the Haast's Eagle had a profound impact on New Zealand's ecosystems. As the top predator, the eagle played a crucial role in controlling the population of large herbivores like the Moa. Its absence likely contributed to changes in the structure of New Zealand's forests and grasslands, as the Moa population declined and other herbivores took their place.

The Haast's Eagle in Maori Culture

The Haast's Eagle continues to be remembered in Maori culture, where it is often associated with legends of giant birds and mythical creatures. The eagle's impressive size and hunting abilities made it a natural subject for folklore, and stories of the "Pouakai" or "Hokioi" have been passed down through generations.

These legends serve as a reminder of the eagle's once-dominant presence in New Zealand's skies and the deep connection between the island's people and its wildlife.

6. Conclusion: The Haast's Eagle— A Lost Giant of New Zealand

The Haast's Eagle was a formidable predator, capable of taking down prey much larger than itself. Its extinction, closely tied to the disappearance of the Moa, represents a tragic loss for New Zealand's unique ecosystems. While the eagle is officially extinct, the occasional reports of large birds and the possibility of de-extinction keep the memory of this giant bird of prey alive.

Whether or not the Haast's Eagle is ever revived or rediscovered, its story highlights the importance of protecting the world's remaining biodiversity and the delicate balance of island ecosystems.

LIVING FOSSILS: SURVIVORS FROM THE DISTANT PAST

T hroughout the history of life on Earth, most species that have ever existed are now extinct. Yet, a few remarkable creatures have survived through millions of years of evolution, earning the title of "living fossils." These species have changed little from their ancient ancestors, offering a glimpse into the deep past. From the Coelacanth, a prehistoric fish once thought extinct, to the Horseshoe Crab, which predates the dinosaurs, these living fossils challenge our understanding of extinction and survival.

In this chapter, we'll explore the world of living fossils, examining how these ancient creatures survived mass extinctions and what their continued existence can teach us about evolution, resilience, and the possibility that other "extinct" species might still survive.

1. What Are Living Fossils?
The term "living fossil" was first coined by Charles Darwin to describe species that have remained largely unchanged over millions of years. These species are considered "relics" of ancient ecosystems, having survived multiple extinction events and

major shifts in the Earth's climate.

Characteristics of Living Fossils

Living fossils are species that exhibit little evolutionary change compared to their ancient ancestors, often retaining primitive traits that have long since disappeared in other species. They are typically found in stable environments, where evolutionary pressures are less intense, allowing them to persist in their original forms.

Some of the most famous living fossils include:

- **Coelacanths:** A deep-sea fish once thought to have gone extinct 66 million years ago, rediscovered alive in 1938 off the coast of South Africa.
- **Horseshoe Crabs:** Marine arthropods that have existed for over 450 million years, predating the dinosaurs.
- **Ginkgo Trees:** A species of tree that has remained largely unchanged for over 200 million years, often referred to as a "living fossil" in the plant kingdom.
- **Nautiluses:** Marine mollusks that have survived for over 500 million years, with little change in their shell structure or anatomy.

2. The Coelacanth: A Fish Out of Time

The Coelacanth (*Latimeria chalumnae*) is one of the most famous examples of a living fossil, often described as a "living dinosaur of the seas." Once believed to have gone extinct at the end of the Cretaceous period, the Coelacanth was rediscovered in 1938, when a live specimen was caught off the coast of South Africa.

Physical Characteristics

The Coelacanth is a large, deep-sea fish that can grow up to 6 feet in length and weigh over 200 pounds. It has a distinctive lobed pectoral fin, which resembles the early limbs of tetrapods, the first land animals. This unique fin structure suggests that the Coelacanth is closely related to the ancestors of all land vertebrates.

Coelacanths are also known for their unusual blue coloration, which helps them blend into the deep-sea environment. Their scales are thick and armored, providing protection from predators in the dark depths of the ocean.

Rediscovery and Scientific Significance

The rediscovery of the Coelacanth in 1938 was one of the most significant zoological discoveries of the 20th century. The fish was found by a South African fisherman and later identified by marine biologist Marjorie Courtenay-Latimer, who recognized its importance as a "living fossil."

The discovery of a living Coelacanth challenged long-held assumptions about extinction and survival, as the species had been thought extinct for tens of millions of years. Since then, additional populations of Coelacanths have been found in the Indian Ocean, near the Comoros Islands and Indonesia.

The Coelacanth's survival offers a unique opportunity for scientists to study a species that has remained largely unchanged for hundreds of millions of years, providing insights into the evolution of vertebrates and the resilience of life in extreme environments.

3. The Horseshoe Crab: A Survivor of the Deep Past

The Horseshoe Crab (*Limulus polyphemus*) is another well-known living fossil, having survived for over 450 million years. Despite its name, the Horseshoe Crab is more closely related to spiders and scorpions than to true crabs. Its ancient lineage dates back to a time before the dinosaurs, and its primitive body plan has changed little over the millennia.

Physical Characteristics

Horseshoe Crabs are characterized by their hard, horseshoe-shaped exoskeleton, long tail spine (or telson), and multiple legs hidden beneath their bodies. They have blue blood due to the presence of copper-based hemocyanin, which allows them to survive in low-oxygen environments.

Horseshoe Crabs are often found along the coastlines of North America and Southeast Asia, where they burrow into the sand and feed on small invertebrates. They are also known for their mass spawning events, in which thousands of Horseshoe Crabs gather on beaches to lay their eggs.

Ecological and Medical Importance
Horseshoe Crabs play a critical role in coastal ecosystems, as their eggs provide an important food source for migratory birds. Additionally, Horseshoe Crabs are of great medical importance due to their blood, which contains a unique substance called Limulus amebocyte lysate (LAL). This substance is used to detect bacterial contamination in vaccines and medical devices, making the Horseshoe Crab a vital resource for human health.

Despite their ancient lineage, Horseshoe Crabs are now facing threats from habitat destruction, overharvesting, and climate change, raising concerns about the future of this living fossil.

4. The Ginkgo Tree: A Living Relic of the Dinosaur Age

The Ginkgo Tree (*Ginkgo biloba*) is often referred to as a "living fossil" in the plant world. Native to China, this tree species has remained virtually unchanged for over 200 million years, making it one of the oldest living tree species on Earth.

Physical Characteristics
The Ginkgo Tree is easily recognizable by its fan-shaped leaves, which turn bright yellow in the fall. It is a slow-growing, long-lived tree, with some individuals living for over 1,000 years. The Ginkgo's reproductive system is also unique, as it produces separate male and female trees, with the female trees bearing seeds that are enclosed in fleshy, foul-smelling fruit.

Cultural and Medicinal Significance
The Ginkgo Tree has been cultivated in China for thousands of years and is often planted in temples and gardens. It is also valued for its medicinal properties, as Ginkgo leaves are used to improve

memory and cognitive function.

The Ginkgo Tree's ability to survive in urban environments and its resistance to pollution have made it a popular choice for planting in cities around the world. Despite its ancient origins, the Ginkgo remains a resilient and adaptable species, capable of thriving in modern landscapes.

5. Nautiluses: Ancient Survivors of the Ocean Depths

Nautiluses are marine mollusks that have survived for over 500 million years, making them one of the oldest living species on Earth. These ancient creatures are often referred to as "living fossils" due to their resemblance to their prehistoric ancestors.

Physical Characteristics

Nautiluses are characterized by their coiled, chambered shells, which they use to control buoyancy as they move through the water. The animal's soft body is housed within the outermost chamber of the shell, while the inner chambers are filled with gas or liquid to help regulate buoyancy.

Nautiluses have dozens of tentacles that they use to capture prey, and their large, prominent eyes are well-adapted to the low-light conditions of the deep sea. Despite their simple body plan, Nautiluses have survived for hundreds of millions of years with little evolutionary change.

Survival in the Modern World

Nautiluses are found in the deep waters of the Indo-Pacific region, where they inhabit coral reefs and seamounts. Their slow reproductive rates and long lifespan make them vulnerable to overfishing, as their shells are highly prized by collectors.

Despite the threats they face, Nautiluses continue to survive in the deep ocean, offering a window into the distant past and the resilience of life in extreme environments.

6. Conclusion: The Lessons of Living Fossils

Living fossils like the Coelacanth, Horseshoe Crab, Ginkgo Tree, and Nautilus provide valuable insights into the history of life on Earth. These ancient species have survived multiple mass extinctions and environmental changes, offering a glimpse into ecosystems that existed millions of years ago.

The continued survival of living fossils challenges our understanding of evolution and extinction, demonstrating that some species are remarkably resilient in the face of changing environments. Their existence also raises questions about whether other "extinct" species, thought to be lost forever, might still survive in remote or unexplored regions of the world.

As we explore the mysteries of extinction and survival, living fossils remind us of the incredible diversity of life on Earth and the importance of protecting the species that have endured for millions of years.

WHAT IF THEY'RE STILL HERE? ETHICAL, ENVIRONMENTAL, AND SCIENTIFIC IMPLICATIONS

T hroughout this book, we've explored numerous species once thought extinct, yet still clinging to existence in the realm of speculation and cryptozoology. From the Thylacine to the Woolly Mammoth, these creatures challenge our perception of extinction. But what happens if we do rediscover one of these "extinct" animals? What are the ethical, environmental, and scientific implications of such a discovery?

In this concluding chapter, we'll explore the potential consequences of rediscovering an extinct species, including the challenges of conservation, the impact on modern ecosystems, and the role of de-extinction technologies. Could the re-emergence of a species change how we view extinction and conservation? And what responsibilities do we hold in protecting these once-lost creatures?

1. The Ethical Implications of Rediscovery

The rediscovery of a species thought to be extinct presents a range of ethical dilemmas. On one hand, such a discovery would be a cause for celebration, offering a rare second chance to protect and conserve a species that was believed lost. On the other hand, the reintroduction of an "extinct" species into modern ecosystems could have unforeseen consequences.

Human Responsibility

If a species like the Thylacine or the Ivory-Billed Woodpecker were rediscovered, we would face the ethical responsibility of protecting these species from further harm. Many species were driven to extinction by human activity, and their rediscovery would offer an opportunity to rectify past mistakes.

However, rediscovery would also raise questions about how to balance conservation efforts with the needs of local communities. For example, reintroducing a large predator like the Thylacine could create conflicts with livestock farmers, who may see the animal as a threat to their livelihoods.

The Role of Zoos and Captive Breeding Programs

One potential solution to the challenges of conserving rediscovered species is the use of zoos and captive breeding programs. These institutions could play a vital role in breeding small populations and reintroducing them into protected habitats.

However, the ethics of captivity must also be considered. While zoos can help save species from extinction, they often struggle to recreate the natural conditions necessary for an animal's well-being. The long-term success of captive breeding programs depends on finding the right balance between captivity and wild reintroduction.

2. The Environmental Impact of Rediscovered Species

The reintroduction of a species into modern ecosystems presents significant environmental challenges. Ecosystems are dynamic and constantly changing, and the reintroduction of a long-lost species could disrupt the delicate balance of species interactions.

Ecosystem Disruption

Many species that have gone extinct played important roles in their ecosystems. For example, the Passenger Pigeon was a key seed disperser and nutrient cycler in North American forests. If a species like the Passenger Pigeon were reintroduced, it could help restore certain ecological functions.

However, ecosystems have changed significantly since the extinction of these species, and their reintroduction could disrupt modern species and food webs. For instance, the reintroduction of a large predator like the Woolly Mammoth or the Pleistocene Cave Lion could create conflicts with existing wildlife and human populations.

Invasive Species Concerns

There is also the risk that a rediscovered species could become invasive in its new environment. If a species is reintroduced into a habitat where it no longer has natural predators or competitors, it could overpopulate and outcompete other species. This has happened in other instances, such as with certain plant and animal species introduced into new ecosystems by humans.

3. Scientific Opportunities and Challenges

The rediscovery of an extinct species would offer an unprecedented scientific opportunity to study species that were previously only known from fossils or historical records. Such a discovery could provide valuable insights into evolution, genetics, and species resilience.

Genetic Research and Biodiversity

One of the most exciting aspects of rediscovering an extinct species is the opportunity to study its genetic makeup. By comparing the DNA of a rediscovered species with that of its closest living relatives, scientists could gain insights into the process of evolution and adaptation.

The rediscovery of a species also raises questions about genetic diversity. Many rediscovered populations are likely to be small and genetically isolated, which could make them vulnerable to inbreeding and disease. Conservation efforts would need to focus on maintaining genetic diversity and ensuring the long-term survival of the species.

De-Extinction and Its Role in Conservation
De-extinction technologies, such as cloning and gene editing, could play a role in the conservation of rediscovered species. If a population is too small to sustain itself, genetic engineering could help boost the population by introducing new genetic material or even by cloning individuals.

However, the use of de-extinction technologies raises ethical and practical questions. While these technologies offer exciting possibilities for bringing back extinct species, they are still in their early stages and come with significant risks.

4. The Role of Cryptozoology in Modern Science
Cryptozoology, the study of hidden or unknown animals, has long been dismissed as pseudoscience. However, the discovery of species once thought extinct, such as the Coelacanth, has given new legitimacy to the idea that "extinct" animals may still survive in remote or unexplored regions.

The Search for Extinct Species
Cryptozoologists have played an important role in keeping the search for extinct species alive. Their persistence in investigating sightings and collecting evidence has helped raise awareness of the possibility that some species may still exist.

While many cryptozoological investigations have been met with skepticism, the discovery of living fossils like the Coelacanth has demonstrated that even the most improbable survival stories can be true. As new technologies, such as environmental DNA (eDNA) sampling, become more widely available, the search for rediscovered species may become more scientific and less speculative.

The rediscovery of an extinct species would be one of the most significant scientific discoveries of the modern era. It would challenge our understanding of extinction, evolution, and conservation, and offer a second chance to protect a species that was once lost.

However, such a discovery would also come with immense ethical, environmental, and scientific challenges. We would need to carefully consider how to balance the protection of rediscovered species with the needs of modern ecosystems and human populations.

DISCLAIMER

This book was written with the assistance of AI technology. The content within is based on a combination of publicly available information, speculative research, and the imaginative exploration of cryptozoology. While every effort has been made to present accurate descriptions and historical references, much of the subject matter involves folklore, eyewitness accounts, and unverified claims.

Readers are encouraged to approach cryptozoology with an open mind, a healthy dose of skepticism, and a sense of curiosity.

This book is intended for educational and entertainment purposes and is not meant to serve as scientific documentation. The use of AI in the creation of this work is to enhance the writing process and compile research but does not substitute for the work of cryptozoologists, scientists, or researchers dedicated to the field.

Printed in Great Britain
by Amazon

61974154R00060